Makeover

D0735630

Other books by Josephine Feeney

So, You Want to be the Perfect Family?

Visit Josephine's website at www.josephinefeeney.co.uk

Makeover Madness

Josephine Feeney

OXFORD
UNIVERSITY PRESS

OXFORD

UNIVERSITY PRESS

Great Clarendon Street, Oxford OX2 6DP

Oxford University Press is a department of the University of Oxford.
It furthers the University's objective of excellence in research, scholarship,
and education by publishing worldwide in
Oxford New York

Auckland Cape Town Dar es Salaam Hong Kong Karachi
Kuala Lumpur Madrid Melbourne Mexico City Nairobi
New Delhi Shanghai Taipei Toronto

With offices in
Argentina Austria Brazil Chile Czech Republic France Greece
Guatemala Hungary Italy Japan Poland Portugal Singapore
South Korea Switzerland Thailand Turkey Ukraine Vietnam

Oxford is a registered trade mark of Oxford University Press
in the UK and in certain other countries

British Library Cataloguing in Publication Data
Data available

ISBN-13: 978-0-19-275296-3
ISBN-10: 0-19-275296-0

3 5 7 9 10 8 6 4

Typeset by Palimpsest Book Production Limited, Polmont, Stirlingshire

Antony Rowe Ltd, Chippenham, Wiltshire

For the children and staff of Christ the King
Catholic School, Leicester and Charnwood
Primary School, Leicester

1

Assemblies

Back to school. A boiling hot September morning—far too summery to be in school. We marched into the hall to bagpipe music, found a space, and sat cross-legged on the hard floor. Mrs Mazurka, our headteacher, clattered down the side of the hall and stepped onto the stage. She clapped her hands once, twice, three times for us all to be quiet. She looked over with irritation towards the teacher operating the stereo system. The bagpipe music ended abruptly, as if someone had strangled the piper. Some of the boys in my class sniggered before Mrs Mazurka fixed them with a silencing stare.

The hall was packed and warm and fidgety. Out of the top hall window I could see a bright blue sky and the shiny, green leaves of the tall playground trees. My mind wandered out of the hall, back to the holidays, thinking about all the blue-sky days we'd had, imagining they would never end.

Mrs Mazurka began to speak. There was good news and bad news, apparently. 'The good news is,' she said, 'it's a new school year and this is going to be the *best ever* for Venus Crescent Primary School. There's a new mobile classroom at the far end of the playground and lots of new children so . . . we're all going to work really hard and make our parents and teachers happy.' What about us being happy? I thought. All this talk about hard work didn't make me happy—it made me want to escape, via the top window and the tall trees, out of there and up to the park.

'Bad news,' Mrs Mazurka said. 'Because of the new classroom and the limited amount of space in the playground there is to be no more football or wild running games. Sorry about that, children.'

Backs straightened, bottoms shuffled, and

heads turned as if we all wanted to say, 'What? Is she serious? What is the point of coming to school if we can't run around and play football at playtime? Get real, Mrs Mazurka!'

I was stiff with pins and needles when I stood to walk out of the hall. Honestly, I'm almost eleven years old and 165 centimetres tall; I shouldn't be sitting cross-legged on a hard wooden floor. I'm too big for that now. (Especially when I'm wearing my summer dress—you can see my pants!) The bagpipe music was much louder as we left the hall and trailed along the corridor, up the stairs to our new classroom.

Mrs Ridley, our teacher, opened the door and marched in confidently. We barged into the room and argued about places, under the teacher's annoyed glare. Mrs Ridley's face rarely changed. As my nan would say, 'Her smiles are as scarce as bank holidays.' I'd watched her in assemblies and on playground duty and her face seemed to be fixed in the same joyless expression. I wasn't looking forward to being in her class. No one ever said, 'Oh, you'll like

Mrs Ridley, she's great fun.' I don't think Mrs Ridley did fun.

Paige beckoned me over to sit next to her. 'Hiya, Leanne!' she said, brightly. 'I love your hair, when did you get it cut?'

'Yesterday,' I replied. 'I'm fed up of ponytails and plaits. I've grown out of them.'

'I'm growing my hair down to my waist,' Paige said. She threw her head back to make her hair appear longer and we giggled. Then we realized that everyone else was quiet and staring at us.

'Thank you, girls,' Mrs Ridley said, sternly. We waited for her to introduce herself, give us a bit of her life story, and tell us the rules of the classroom, that sort of thing. But she was totally silent for a few moments, staring at each of us as if she was counting heads. Then she began speaking. 'Now, I want you all to settle down and copy the title "THE BEST DAY OF MY HOLIDAY" from the board. Then I want you to write about it.'

Straight into work, no buffer zone or anything. What a start to the new school year.

2

Lessons

Shamir's hand shot into the air. 'Miss,' he called. 'We've already done this.'

'No you haven't,' Mrs Ridley retorted. 'You've only been in my classroom ten minutes.'

'No, I mean we did it last year, in Mrs Marsh's class,' Shamir explained.

'Well, you can do it *again*, this year.'

'But that's a bit . . .' Shamir began.

'Get on with it,' Mrs Ridley said, pointing a silencing finger at Shamir.

'I can't remember nowt,' Finlay admitted. A few of us sniggered. Finlay can never remember anything.

'Neither can I,' Shamir agreed.

Mrs Ridley took a deep breath and glared at

us. 'How is it,' she began, 'that I can remember my family holiday in Mablethorpe when I was three years old and yet . . . some of you are unable or *unwilling* to remember what you did last week, or the week before!' It was very hard to imagine Mrs Ridley as a small child, playing by the seaside.

'We never went nowhere,' Paige added.

'Me neither,' I said.

'What's Mablethorpe?' Shamir asked. 'Is it abroad?'

'No, it's the seaside,' Finlay said, smiling. 'We went there once.'

Mrs Ridley shook her head in disgust and then she rapped her knuckles against the whiteboard. 'Come on,' she nagged. 'Get on with it.'

I wrote the title, underlined it three times and drew flowers around it as I was thinking. There had been lots of brilliant days this holiday so which one should I write about? I looked up and noticed that Paige was busy scribbling away so I started writing:

THE BEST DAY OF MY HOLIDAY

We never went nowhere for our holiday this year because my dad wanted to do the bathroom up. It looks brilliant now.

The best day of my holiday was when I got up about half eight and I switched on the telly in our front room. There was this competition about school and you had to write a letter and say why your school was the worst in the country. A few days later when I was watching the telly again, the presenter said, 'Are you there, Leanne King?' and I nearly fainted. I shouted my dad and we were jumping around and whooping and everything. They liked my idea best so I won a rucksack and lots of other goodies like this pen I'm writing with. I felt really excellent when my name flashed up on the screen—sort of famous.

They asked me lots of questions about our school. And my letter went through to the sort of final. It's for this new series that's going to be on telly soon. About

Perfect Schools. (It would be brill if they chose our school for it.) After that I played out on my scooter with my mates from our street. We went up the park and we went on the BMX course. I fell off twice. It was a laugh. Then I went home for my tea. We had sausages.

I drew a picture underneath the last sentence (of me falling off my scooter) just as the bell rang for playtime. Mrs Ridley spoke again in a very stern voice. 'Remember! No charging around the playground and no football!' We all groaned together.

Back to boring, *boring* school.

In case you're wondering, this is the letter I wrote about our school:

Dear Producer,

     I am writing to tell you all about my school for the PERFECT SCHOOL competition. My school is absolutely ancient. It was actually built centuries ago and it looks like an old factory from the outside.

Inside our school the classrooms haven't been decorated since Victorian times—you can tell from the colours of the paint and the big cupboards along the corridor. Outside, the playground is very small. My nan says that it was built for when children behaved themselves and were polite and not as boisterous as we are. Do you know the sort of children I mean? They walked around playing with spinning tops and hopscotch and leapfrog. I've seen pictures of the children then. They all looked very well behaved in their frilly dresses with white aprons and their hair tied back in silky ribbons. Nowadays, we get in one another's way all the time and we're always falling out in the playground. That's because it's too small.

Then there's our teachers; they are like Victorians, too, like the ones in the photos, never smiling, always looking grumpy or angry. And the *clothes* they wear! Honestly, sometimes I feel like saying to them, 'Have you looked in a mirror this morning?' And the dinner lady is on the verge of a nervous breakdown every day. She looks like one of those old Victorian ladies in a long black dress, who always needs smelling salts. Talking of smells—our school dinners are the most disgusting plates of slop ever. They are like Victorian bowls of gruel!

I have got some brilliant ideas for turning our school into the Perfect School. I watch all those makeover programmes on telly and my nan buys all the magazines for doing up old houses. She lives just around the corner from school and her house is like a little palace.

There are lots of things that need changing and sorting out in our school and it would be so brilliant if you could come in and make us into a Perfect School.

Yours most sincerely,

Leanne King

3

Dinners

At dinner time, Finlay ran out to the playground with his ball. He started kicking it
around. Mrs Towers blew her whistle and then
pointed at him. Finlay picked up the ball and
turned to face her, looking puzzled. 'What?' he
shouted.

Mrs Towers went mad. 'Get here!' she yelled.
Finlay shuffled over towards her. 'What do you
think you're playing at?'

'Football,' Finlay replied honestly.

'Don't be so cheeky,' Mrs Towers retorted.
'I'm not being . . .'

'You are,' Mrs Towers said, pointing at him.
'You think you can do as you please out here.'

'I don't,' Finlay replied.

11

'You've been told: *no football!*'

'Oh,' Finlay sighed, gradually remembering Mrs Mazurka's words. 'I forgot.'

'Well, you can go and stand over there by the fence and remember,' Mrs Towers said.

Mrs Towers is our dinner lady, otherwise known as the Midday Supervisor, and she behaves like a nervous zoo keeper, who's always expecting the animals to attack. When she walks into our playground she rolls up her sleeves and scowls at us, daring us to misbehave or step a foot out of place. Paige knows somebody who lives next door to her and she says that Mrs Towers makes Mr Towers stand against the fence when he doesn't do as he's told.

I think that she hates being a dinner lady and she seems to hate children. Once I asked her why she worked in our school and she said that it gets her out of the house. (So do floods and fire, my nan says.) Nan also says that dinner ladies are badly paid for a hard job and that's why they're often cranky with the kids.

Anyway, Finlay stood against the fence and the rest of us walked around the playground like old folk strolling along the prom at Skegness. Eventually, Paige and I sat in the grey concrete corner of the playground, moaning about being back at boring, boring school. 'Look at it, Paige,' I said.

'I know, Leanne, it's a disgrace,' Paige replied.

'It'd be brilliant if we won that Perfect School competition,' I said.

'Oh yeah,' Paige said. 'What did it feel like when you saw your name on telly?'

'Fantastic!' I said. I sighed at the lovely memory of that morning and then we stared up at the red brick building. Our classroom is two floors up, just under the carved stone date, 1878. I wondered about all the children who had played in this playground. Did they feel the same as we do? Were they hoping for a Perfect School?

My stomach began to seriously rumble with hunger just as Mrs Towers blew the whistle for us to line up quickly in our class groups. When we filed into the dining room, I suddenly lost my appetite, as usual. The smell! Whatever they were cooking, it smelt as though it had been soaked first in soap suds and vinegar.

Mrs Whitburn, the cook, was dishing up with two other ladies. Last term she'd bought a big chalkboard, like they have in cafés, and she wrote 'Whitburn's Bistro' at the top and underneath, 'Today's Specials'. On this particular day she had written *Chicken Chickettes* and *Turkey Surprise*. Something else had been rubbed out.

'What about me?' Shamir asked, as he pushed his tray along the counter. 'I'm vegetarian.'

'You weren't last term,' Mrs Whitburn said, briskly, without lifting her eyes from the passing trays. 'Manners!' she warned those who forgot to express their gratitude for the pickled washing-up suds.

'I was! I've always been veggie and anyway I didn't stay to dinner last term,' Shamir protested. 'Where's the veggie option?'

'Well, you can have the Turkey Surprise,' Mrs Whitburn suggested.

'Turkey's meat,' Shamir said. He folded his arms in protest and tried to stop anyone else passing by.

Mrs Whitburn leaned right over the metal

counter and put her face close to Shamir's. She always does this when she's challenged. 'Well, the surprise is, my little *vegetarian*,' she whispered, 'there's hardly any turkey in it! Now, do you want potato smileys?'

Shamir stomped over to the table and practically threw his tray down next to mine. 'Turkey surprise!' he complained. 'More like tortured tatties and mashed monkey!'

Children on the tables nearby shuffled around to examine Shamir's dinner. Their chairs scraped along the noisy floor as they moved. 'Turn around!' Mrs Towers ordered.

'It's a disgrace,' Paige said, fidgeting restlessly on her chair. 'No vegetarian stuff for Shamir.'

'I'm going back on packed lunches,' Shamir announced.

'Dining rooms are for *eating*, not *talking*,' Mrs Towers called, pointing over at our table. 'Come on—belt up and eat up!' Me and Paige tutted loudly. Although we had stopped talking, the noise level in the dining room grew and grew for several minutes as children raised their voices to make themselves heard. Mrs Towers started flapping her arms about as if she was trying to extinguish a forest fire.

I sat quietly chewing my disgusting Chicken Chickettes which were only second cousin to any kind of meat. The potato smileys were frowning and the peas and carrots were cold and tasteless. I gazed around the dining room at the chipping paintwork and the fading posters encouraging us to eat healthily. I leaned over to Paige. 'Wouldn't it be brilliant,' I said, 'if we got made into the Perfect School on telly?'

'Yeah,' Paige said brightly. 'Fingers crossed, Leanne.'

'Eat!' Mrs Towers shouted. She looked directly at our table. For a split second there was no talking in the whole of the dining room. Even the knives and forks were silenced. Mrs Whitburn and her team were clanging and banging about as they cleared the huge steel pots from the serving station. After a few moments the quiet hum of conversation returned.

'I said, *eat!*' Mrs Towers insisted. She pointed at our table again and wiggled her arm about, looking like an angry elephant rather than a nervous zookeeper. I looked at Paige and noticed that all her fingers were crossed. I crossed mine, too, and whispered a wish. *'Please, please, please choose us for the Perfect School and sort out Mrs Towers before she drives us all mad!'*

4

Headteachers

It was unbearably hot in our room under the roof that day. I could already feel that it would be a long, bad-tempered sort of afternoon. There were no displays on the wall so there was nothing to look at but the heavy beams bisecting the room.

During the lunch break, Mrs Ridley had reorganized the furniture in the room and placed name labels on each table. I was on Table T with Paige (thank goodness), Finlay, and Shamir. As soon as we settled at our table, Mrs Ridley called, 'Leanne . . . I want you to take your work down to the Head and give her this note . . .' She scribbled a few words on a piece of sugar paper, folded it several times and handed it to me.

Why? I thought but I didn't say.

'And you, Finlay, Paige, and Shamir.' We all looked at one another, puzzled. 'Off you go.' She handed us our work and we left the room and walked down the echoing staircase to Mrs Mazurka's office. The shiny pale blue walls felt cool in the heat of the day.

'What've I done wrong now?' Finlay asked.

'Nothing,' Shamir replied. 'She probably thinks our work is very good so she wants to show it to . . .'

Finlay suddenly stopped, as if rooted to the spot. 'Why don't you read the note?' he suggested.

'No!' Paige warned. 'It's *private*.' She started to walk faster.

'It's not in an envelope,' Shamir observed. He ran ahead of Paige and then turned to face her, walking backwards.

'I suppose it would be all right, Paige. She won't know we've read it,' I said, hurrying to catch up with my friend.

'Well, I think that's very rude,' Paige said, grumpily.

'Go on, read it,' Finlay urged.

I unfolded the note as we walked along. 'It says, *Dear Maddy . . .*'

'Maddy! More like *Mad* Mazurka!' Finlay giggled, jumping up and down. 'Mad Mazurka!'

'Don't be so immature, Finlay,' Paige snapped, staring at Finlay. 'Anyway, why are you wearing your trainers? You'll get done for that.'

'It's OK,' Finlay said. 'They're not mine, they're Shamir's.'

'What?' Paige said, looking very puzzled. Then she rushed off again.

'Slow down, Paige,' I said. 'Listen to this: *Trying to avoid problems before they arise as you suggested in our Teacher Day yesterday. These characters have all produced subversive essays this morning . . .*'

'What's subversive?' Shamir asked, looking at me as if I might know the answer.

'Ain't it like a boat that goes under water,' Finlay replied.

'That's a submarine, you idiot!' Paige hissed.

I folded the note quickly as we neared Mrs Mazurka's office.

She was sitting at her desk, with the door open. 'Nice to see you all on the first day back,' she said. I handed her the note and then stood back with the others against her bookcase. She read it quickly. 'Now,' she said, a bit too brightly for my liking, 'I'd like you to read out what you've written for your very first piece of work for your Mrs Ridley. Who's going to go first?'

We all stared at her, shuffled a bit, and then nudged one another. Finlay was beginning to look desperate. 'You go first, Leanne,' he muttered.

'Thanks for volunteering, Finlay,' Mrs Mazurka said. 'Off you go.'

Finlay stared at his work for a few seconds. I knew he found it hard to read his own writing. Then he began. *'The best day of my holiday . . . was when we was fling . . .'*

'What?' Mrs Mazurka interrupted. 'Do you mean you were *flung*?'

Shamir started to giggle.

'No . . . we was *flying* back from . . .'

'Why didn't you say that?' Mrs Mazurka asked.

'Because you told me to read what I writ . . .'

'What I wrote,' Mrs Mazurka corrected Finlay. He looked totally puzzled. 'Carry on.'

'*We was fling back from Florida,*' Finlay continued, '. . . *and these two old birds started fighting and it was cool like something off the telly one of them was dead posh like Mrs Mazurka and the other was dead common saying you ain't sitting here and all that and it was a right laugh but they wouldn't sit down so we had to go to Maine which is a funny name for a place and we stayed there for the night and I had a burger and chips and then I went to bed and that was the best day of my holiday.*'

'Thank you, Finlay,' Mrs Mazurka said. 'And by the way, why are you wearing your trainers? You know they're not allowed in class.'

'It's all right, Miss. They're not mine, they're Shamir's,' Finlay replied.

Mrs Mazurka looked totally confused. Then she shook her head and said, 'Who's going to go next?'

'I'll go,' Shamir volunteered. '*The best day of my holiday was when my mum and dad told me* that we was going to India for six weeks in November because it is cheaper then. I will miss my mate Finlay but I was pleased because it will mean that I get away from school and doing stupid, boring exercises like writing about the best day of my holiday again when we have already done it in Mrs Marsh's class and I am extremely bored with doing the same thing again.'

'Well done, Shamir,' Mrs Mazurka said, only she didn't look as though she meant it. 'Paige?'

'Do I have to, Miss?' Paige asked.

'Yes—you do,' Mrs Mazurka replied.

Paige cleared her throat. '*The best day of my holiday,*' she read, hesitantly, '*was when I was playing out with my mates and this bulldozer came down our street and the driver asked us the way to the old steel warehouse and I said, go to the bottom of the road and turn left it's straight ahead you can't miss it and when he had gone one of my friends said you've sent him the wrong way but I said, no, he will think our school is the old warehouse and he will knock it down and then a few minutes later we heard an enormous crash because he had demolished the school. Hooray!*'

'Very interesting, Paige,' Mrs Mazurka said, flatly.

'I made it up—it's not true, only we never did much in the holidays and we never went nowhere,' Paige explained, unnecessarily. She was twirling a tendril of her long hair as she spoke and sort of turning away from me, Shamir, and Finlay.

'We didn't go *anywhere*, Paige,' Mrs Mazurka corrected her.

'Didn't you, Miss?' Paige said, gently.

'I am correcting your *English*, Paige, not telling you about my summer!' Mrs Mazurka explained. 'And now it's your turn, Leanne.'

I read my story slowly. I glanced up at Mrs Mazurka's face when I said about the worst school in the country. Now she was wearing an expression that could turn the milk sour, as my nan would say. I felt hot and nervous. She looked as though she was about to explode. I finished reading and my paper fluttered as my hand gently shook, waiting for Mrs Mazurka's response.

5

Corridors

Mrs Mazurka didn't shout at us. She looked quite sad, actually. 'You know, kids,' she began, 'when I became headteacher at this school five years ago, I had high hopes for you all and for the buildings and the grounds . . .' Her voice sort of trailed off and she stared out of the window, on to the main road and the railway line.

That was true. I remembered when she started. She had long, jet-black, curly hair and she was always rushing around, smiling, in cool short skirts and high heels. She used to play the guitar and teach us new songs on Friday afternoons. But that's all gone—her hair, her cool clothes, and her singing. Now, she looks more like someone who works in a bank with her smart suits, flat shoes, and short hair and she always looks so tired and pale, even after the summer holiday.

'I never thought,' she continued, 'that I would have children saying that they wanted the school *demolished*!' She took a deep breath. 'Is it really that bad?' Nobody answered. Paige, Finlay, and Shamir looked at the floor whilst I looked out of the window and watched a passenger train slip over the railway bridge next to the school. The building shook. 'And I had such *high* hopes for this year!'

For a few moments there was an embarrassing silence. I could hear the voices of teachers in faraway classrooms shouting out, '*Do you mind?*' or '*I have told you about twenty times.*' Their words bounced and echoed along the shiny walls of the corridors, down into Mrs Mazurka's office.

'If none of you are going to say anything, you might as well go back to class,' Mrs Mazurka said.

As soon as we turned away from her office door and started to walk slowly up the stairs,

Shamir began, 'You shouldn't have said that about the school being rubbish, Leanne.'

'Oh, pardon me, Mr Perfect,' I replied. 'I was just making it up to win a competition, *actually*.'

'And you,' Shamir said, nudging Paige. 'Shouldn't have been so nasty, getting that bulldozer to . . .'

'It was a story, duh!' Paige sneered. 'And don't poke me!' She pushed Shamir against the pale blue wall.

'Leave Shamir alone,' Finlay warned. 'You shouldn't push people around like that. You think you know it all, Paige.'

'And you know *nothing*!' Paige moved towards Finlay, standing too close to him. 'And you're not supposed to wear trainers in school.'

'I told you they're . . . are you calling me thick?' Finlay asked, suddenly realizing what Paige had said.

'Well, it wasn't me who was *fling* home from America, was it?' Paige remarked.

'That's a bit unfair, Paige,' I said. 'We all make mistakes and you know that Finlay does some-times struggle with his writing.'

'Well, as a matter of fact . . .' Finlay began, but he wasn't able to finish his sentence because Mrs Ridley walked out onto the top landing. She placed her hands on her hips and glared at us.

'I *hate* to interrupt your group discussion,' she said. 'But *we* cannot concentrate because of the noise.'

'Sorry, Miss,' I said and walked quickly into the room, followed by the others. I felt angry. I don't like it when teachers are sarcastic.

'We're doing science,' she announced. 'There's a worksheet on your desk.' We trooped in and collapsed into our chairs. I used the worksheet as a fan and looked over at Paige who copied me. She raised her eyes to the ceiling. I could see the pearls of sweat on her forehead.

'Miss, what do we have to do?' Finlay asked, more flustered than ever. He used the sleeve of his T-shirt to wipe the moisture from his brow and his head.

'Complete the worksheet,' she responded in a mechanical voice.

'But I don't know how to,' Finlay said,

shuffling in his chair, lifting his top away from the sweat and heat of his back.

'If you'd been here you would know what to do,' Mrs Ridley said.

'You sent me to . . .' Finlay continued, looking puzzled.

'Well, I hope you've learned your lesson,' Mrs Ridley said, folding her arms and gazing at Finlay over the rims of her spectacles. Finlay looked perplexed. Shamir shuffled closer to his side of the table and tried to explain what we had to do.

Mrs Ridley sat at her desk and massaged just above the bridge of her nose. My nan does that when she's really stressed. I had an idea. 'Miss?' I raised my hand. 'When it was this hot last year, Mrs Marsh used to take us out to the playground to sit under the horse chestnut tree to cool off. She said it cleared our heads.'

'Well . . . this is *not* last year, Leanne, and I am *not* Mrs Marsh,' she said. 'And we are *not* going anywhere.'

I looked at Paige and we shrugged our shoulders. Unless something very dramatic happened, this was going to be one very long, difficult year.

6
Letters

Then something very dramatic did happen.

Seven o'clock the next morning, in my strawberry-pink bedroom, I could hear Dad pottering about singing along to the radio and shouting, 'Leanne? Are you up?'

Then the clunk of the letter box as the postwoman made her delivery. Dad wandered into the hall. 'Leanne!' he called again. I could hear him groan as he bent down to pick up the letters. (He needs to lose some weight.) Then, suddenly, he really started yelling.

'Leanne!'

'I'm up!' I called back, even though I wasn't. I started searching for my uniform under the pile of clothes at the end of my bed.

'There's a letter for you,' he said as he started to run up the stairs. 'It's from the Kids Broadcasting Company, the KBC!'

I kicked the bedclothes back and ran out on to our lime-green landing. 'Let's have a look,' I said. I was dead excited. Dad passed the letter up and sat down on the middle stair.

'It's from the KBC, Dad!'

'I know, it's on the envelope!' Dad replied. 'What does it say?'

'It says, *Dear Leanne* . . .'

'*There's* a surprise.'

'*After careful consideration*, blah, blah, blah and all that stuff . . .'

'Yes—get to the point, Leanne.'

'*We think that your school has superb potential for transforming into the Perfect School. It has crumbling, inadequate buildings, teachers who seem to be finding it hard to cope, and support workers who might benefit from a huge moraley boost* . . .'

'Morale,' Dad interrupted.

'Whatever . . . *So congratulations, Leanne! To help us transform yours into the Perfect School, would you please fill in the enclosed application form and send it to us in the envelope attached. We look forward to hearing from you soon, with best wishes, Evergreen* . . . something unpronounceable, *Research Assistant, Perfect Schools.'*

I clutched the letter to my chest. 'It's like a dream come true, Dad.' I closed my eyes and imagined myself at the school entrance, smiling at the camera and saying, 'Welcome to our school. Come and see how bad it really is.' Like in those programmes where they show you a crumbling building, looking all derelict and then, bit by bit, they make it much better. And it always looks dead simple. Everyone in the country would see me standing there, talking about . . .

'D'you want porridge or cornflakes?' Dad asked, cutting into my dream.

'What?'

'Porridge or cornflakes?'

'I'm too excited to eat, Dad,' I replied.

'Listen, Leanne: if you're going to create the perfect school, you need some breakfast!'

7

Playgrounds

In my excitement I ran all the way to school and searched for Paige in the playground. I ran over to greet her and pushed the letter from the KBC into her hands. 'Read this!'

A moment later she leapt into the air. 'This is amazing, Leanne! We're going to be famous, me and you,' she yelped. A small crowd began to gather around us, attracted by Paige's excitement. Finlay and Shamir edged towards us.

'What you looking at?' Finlay asked, leaning over Paige's shoulder.

'We're going to be on telly,' Paige said, jumping about.

'What—on *Crimewatch*?' Finlay suggested.

'No!' I said, holding the letter out for Finlay to read.

'My Uncle Ned was on that,' Finlay said.

'And did they catch him?' Paige questioned.

'He's a detective, duh!' Finlay retorted.

'Anyway, why are you going to be on telly, Leanne?' Shamir asked.

'So that . . .' I began, opening my arms out wide like an enthusiastic television presenter. 'We can become *the* . . . Perfect School!'

'Well, you'll have to get rid of all the teachers first,' Shamir suggested, shoving his hands into his trouser pockets.

'And the dinner ladies,' Finlay added, gazing over towards the dining room.

'And the cooks,' Paige agreed, putting her arm around my shoulders.

'Then knock it all down,' Shamir continued, 'and start building some place else.'

'Hey, that was my idea!' Paige protested, nudging Shamir.

'Like the seaside—build it at the seaside!' Finlay said, waving his elbows about and putting his thumbs in the air.

'Nathan would have a long way to go home for his dinner,' Shamir said, chuckling.

'We have to make a list of suggestions,' I said, 'for the KBC.'

'Let's do it at playtime,' Paige suggested.

'I'll help,' Finlay volunteered, looking ready and enthusiastic.

'We don't want any *boys*, thank you,' Paige said, snootily.

'Why not?' Finlay questioned, his shoulders slumped forward.

'Yeah, you're not allowed to exclude boys, it's against the law,' Shamir said. 'And stop being so nasty to Finlay, Paige. You've really got it in for him this year.'

'Well, I think it's best if Finlay and Shamir help,' I decided. 'We're all on the same table so it'll be easy to do it during quiet reading time.'

'Are you serious, Leanne?' Paige asked. 'She won't let us talk in *discussion* time so she'll hardly let us talk in *quiet reading* time—especially if Shamir and Finlay misbehave, as usual.' Paige glared at the two boys.

'What are you on about,' Shamir said. 'I'm always good in class.'

'No you're not, Shamir,' Paige argued. 'You're—'

'I am!' Shamir insisted.

'So am I,' Finlay agreed. 'I can't help it if—'

'Listen!' I interrupted. 'What we'll do is this—you write down some suggestions on rough paper, pass them to me, and . . .' Mrs Ridley walked into the centre of the playground and blew the whistle for the start of the day. At that moment, we were supposed to stop talking and stand still. But I was so excited that I didn't and I was the only person in the whole of the junior playground who was talking. '. . . then I'll write a letter this evening with all your—'

'Leanne King!' Mrs Ridley called. She didn't have to shout all that loud because there was absolute silence in the playground. 'What a start to the day! Now get into your class lines and lead into school. Mrs Marsh's class first.'

I clutched the KBC letter to my chest and looked at Paige. She smiled.

School could only get better.

8

Changes

VENUS CRESCENT SCHOOL

10th September

Dear Evergreen,

Thank you for your letter. I have filled in the application form with all the stuff about our school and this is the extra information you asked for. The people who are going to be in my team are Paige, who's my best friend, and Shamir and Finlay. We are all on table T in our class. We have had a chat today and when our teacher wasn't looking we wrote a list of the things that need changing.

This is what we want to change. We would like:

1. New teachers! Mrs Ridley, our class teacher, is the grumpiest grunt in the whole of civilization. We want someone who likes a bit of fun and who . . . smiles. It's not too much to ask, is it? While you're at it, you could get rid of Mrs Mazurka too. She's not old but she's become very bo-ring and she gives us long dreary lectures in assembly. Which brings me on to number 2 . . .

2. Better assemblies with cool music and also chairs for the Year 6 kids to sit on so that when we go into assembly we don't have to be all squashed up.

3. A new dinner lady! The one we've got at the moment is on the waiting list for a nervous breakdown so we'd like somebody who is calm and chilled and relaxed. It would be nice to have a dinner lady who doesn't go ballistic and explode if we do the tiniest thing wrong. And then we'd like . . .

4. A new cook! Most of the kids in this school are hungry every afternoon because they know that the cook is trying to poison us with her recipes. Honestly, Evergreen, the food is pure disgusting.

5. Will you do something about our dining room? It's a total and utter disgrace and even if we did have tasty and non-toxic food, the state of the dining room puts you off eating.

6. We also need a massive, industrial strength extractor fan to take the evil smells out of the dining room.

7. A new classroom! It is the worst one in the world because it hasn't been painted for about a hundred years and we have to climb two sets of steep stone steps to reach it.

8. A bigger playground where we can run around and have proper games without being told off.

9. An outdoor area for lessons so that when it's boiling hot we can sit outside.

10. A different view from the playground. All we can see are houses, factories, and the railway line and we really do get tired of seeing the same thing day after day.

I hope this is what you want, Evergreen. We can think of lots of other things that need doing but Paige says it's best if we stick to just ten because you might be able to do two a day.

I hope you like our ideas for making Venus Crescent into the most Perfect School in the world.

Yours most sincerely,

Leanne King

PS You won't show my letter to anyone at school, will you?

16th September

Dear Leanne,

Phew! That is some wish list! Leanne, I have a feeling that Venus Crescent is going to be an absolutely *brilliant* project and a lot of that will be down to *your* tremendous efforts.

Leanne, you have worked *incredibly* hard on this already so it's important for you to understand that although we will do our very best to transform your school, we simply cannot put right *all* that is wrong. We really need to pare down your list, in a manner of speaking.

So . . . let's get thinking again and next week when I visit your school, you can finally decide how we can turn Venus Crescent into the *Perfect School*!

With very best wishes,

Evergreen

41

9
Problems

A few days later, at the end of another unbeliev-ably boring assembly, Mrs Mazurka announced my name. I didn't hear her at first. I had switched off when Mrs Mazurka was encouraging us to be kind to old people and help cats and dogs cross the road. Or it might have been the other way around.

Paige nudged me. 'Leanne,' she whispered. 'She's talking to you.'

'Yes, Miss?' I asked, quickly.

'Come to my office immediately after assembly,' she said, in a strangely clipped voice.

'Naughty, naughty,' Finlay sniggered as he tutted and waved a finger in front of me.

'I wonder what's up?' I whispered to Paige, ignoring Finlay's taunts.

A few minutes later I was standing in Mrs Mazurka's office. 'The last time I saw you here, Leanne, you read a story about Venus Crescent being the worst school in the country.' She paused, taking a deep breath. 'Then . . . yesterday I had a phone call from somebody called *Evergreen*.'

'Oh, great,' I said. 'She's the one from the KBC. Did she say when they were starting?' I asked.

'She rang,' Mrs Mazurka said quietly, 'to ask for my permission.'

'Oh, brilliant,' I said, smiling.

'Which I haven't given . . .' She paused. My heart sank and my smile drooped. Then she added, '. . . yet.'

'Why not?' I asked.

'Because I need to know what *exactly* is going on before I allow any television company access to our school.'

'But it's the *KBC*, Miss,' I explained.

'I don't care if it's Buckingham Palace

Television. What kind of message does it present to parents if we let television cameras in to reveal all the problems in our school which I have laboured to solve over the last few years?'

'Sorry, Miss,' I said. 'I didn't think of it like that. I just thought it would be a brilliant thing for the school.'

She sat behind her desk staring at me. In the hall I could hear Mrs Marsh arriving with her plimsolled class. *'Get down!'* she called. *'The wall bars are not for climbing!'*

'Do you honestly believe that, Leanne?' Mrs Mazurka asked in a gentler tone of voice.

'Yes,' I replied.

'Find a space,' Mrs Marsh commanded.

'PE again,' Mrs Mazurka sighed, shaking her head. 'It drives *me* up the wall.'

'I said, find a space, Milli-Mae, not a curtain!' Mrs Marsh roared.

'It's not your fault that the school's like this, Miss,' I persuaded. Nan would have been proud of me.

Mrs Mazurka stared at the papers on her desk for a few moments. 'No,' she said. 'You're right,

Leanne. It isn't my fault. I have done my best and there's only so much you can do even though I seem to have worked twenty-five hours every day over the last few years . . .'

'I know, Mrs Mazurka,' I said, trying to get round her.

I could see that Mrs Mazurka was considering it seriously. Then suddenly, she smiled. 'Oh, why not, Leanne,' she said, removing her glasses. 'Let's give it a go.'

I don't know what changed her mind. I'd like to think it was me being understanding and considerate. Nan says that gets you a long way. Whatever it was, I skipped and jumped along the corridor on my way back to class. 'Yes!' I cried. 'I've done it!'

```
Venus  Crescent  Primary  School
        Venus  Crescent
       Universe  Estate
         Leicester
```

September 22nd

Dear Parents,

We are just over halfway through our first month back at school so I feel I should thank you for your co-operation in helping us settle back into a new academic year. September is always an exciting and challenging time, none more so than this year. The Kids Broadcasting Company, KBC, has expressed a desire to do some preliminary research and filming in Venus Crescent School within the next two weeks. We need your permission for this to happen. If you agree to the filming, please complete the slip below and return it to school by **September 27th**.

Yours faithfully,

Mrs M. Mazurka
Headteacher

I do/do not give permission for

Name ....Class.....................

to be filmed by Kids Broadcasting Company.

Signed[Parent/Guardian].....................Date........

10

Evergreen

Me and Paige were very surprised when
Evergreen arrived at school the following
Tuesday. For days we had talked and speculated
about her appearance. 'I bet she's tall and
willowy with long, blonde hair,' Paige said.
'She probably wears designer clothes and
high-heeled shoes.'

'I think she's got jet black hair and she ties it
up into one of those sort of rolls whilst she's
working and . . .' I said.

'She's probably covered in leaves,' Finlay
interrupted.

'And needles and pine cones,' Shamir added
and then he and Finlay swung back on their chairs
and giggled until Mrs Ridley glared at them.

'What are you on about?' Paige whispered.

'Evergreen!' Shamir and Finlay said together. 'Trees?' they added, noticing Paige's puzzled expression.

'Oh!' Paige rolled her eyes and sighed. 'You shouldn't make fun of people's names.'

I knew why she said that. When Paige first arrived at our school, in Year Three, Finlay asked her, 'Where did your mum and dad get a name like that from?' and Paige replied, very quickly, 'Out of a book!'

Anyway, when Evergreen arrived she wasn't tall, willowy, and blonde with designer clothes nor did she wear her long, black hair in a roll. She was small, with curly ginger hair, a beaming smile, and she was brimming with energy and enthusiasm.

We met her in Mrs Mazurka's office. 'Great to meet you at long last, Leanne,' she said. 'And you Paige, Shamir, and Finlay.'

I suddenly felt a bit shy and tongue-tied so I was relieved when Mrs Mazurka said, 'And we're delighted to have you here, Evergreen.' Mrs Mazurka was all bubbly and bright, for a change. 'Now then, Evergreen wants a tour of the school so . . .'

'We'll take her,' Finlay volunteered.

'That would be lovely! I'd like to see your classroom first,' Evergreen said. 'And then the playground and the dining room and . . .'

We started the tour of school just as the bell rang for playtime. Children poured out of classrooms and started to chase down the corridor. They spotted Evergreen, slowed down and stared at her as they moved along. Then the questions started. 'Who's she?'

'Who's that?'

'What's she doing here?'

'Is she from the telly?' one of the Year Threes asked me. Word had spread around that there were going to be television cameras in school. Evergreen waved and smiled at him.

'Is it starting today?' another boy asked, holding up a crowd of children. Behind him, somebody pushed.

'Get a move on!' they yelled.

Evergreen was carrying a small camcorder and a digital camera hung from her neck. Every few seconds she filmed some of the children. One or two jumped up and down, waved their hands and mouthed, 'Hello, Mum!' Evergreen waved back. 'I'm not your mum,' she said, brightly.

Paige led the way up the two flights of stairs to our classroom. 'It's very unusual for a school to be built on three floors,' Evergreen said.

'It's Victorian, you know,' Shamir said.

'Yes, I remember Leanne's original letter,' Evergreen said.

'It's that old it's probably best just to knock it down and start all over again,' Finlay suggested.

'Oh no, no!' Evergreen protested. 'It has great character; that's why it's going to be such a brilliant project.' Then we walked into the classroom. Evergreen threw her arms out as if she was meeting someone off a train. 'Wow!' she cried. 'I love this room.'

'What?' Finlay asked. 'Well, I *don't*!'

'I hate it,' Shamir added.

'What's wrong with the room, lads?' Evergreen asked. 'It isn't that bad.' She turned towards Finlay, filming his response.

'One—I'm no good at nothing,' Finlay listed, pointing to his index finger. Then he chuckled. 'I can't talk when you're doing that.'

'Sorry, I'll switch it off for a minute,' Evergreen said.

'Right . . . and two, we've got the most mardy, miserable teacher in the whole of the world,' Finlay added.

'She can't stand our table,' Shamir said. 'I think she's called it table T for troublemakers.'

'That's interesting,' Evergreen said. She snapped different views of the room with her camera. 'What about you, Paige and Leanne? How do you feel about this room?'

'It gets very hot in here,' I said.

'It's murder in the afternoons,' Paige agreed.

'I can see all that, kids, but I reckon this room has *fantastic* potential,' Evergreen suggested.

'You *serious?*' Finlay asked.

'Oh yes,' Evergreen said, swinging around, filming every wall and corner of the room.

'And I bet that your teacher has great potential, too,' Evergreen said, 'Once we've given her . . .'

'The sack?' Shamir suggested.

'Yeah,' Finlay agreed and they giggled together.

'You should be careful, she might hear you,' Paige said.

'No . . . a makeover,' Evergreen said. 'Anyway, I want to see your playground *and* your dining room and meet the famous cook.'

'You must be mad,' Finlay said.

Evergreen smiled. 'You have to be just a *little* strange to work in television!'

11
Plans

When the next letter arrived, I gathered Paige, Shamir, and Finlay into the concrete corner of the playground before we had to file into school.

'Look,' I said. 'We've had a really brilliant letter from Evergreen.'

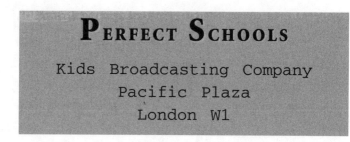

29th September

Dear Leanne,

I'm so excited about this project, I can hardly wait . . . this is going to be *the most* Perfect School! And this is what we're going to do:

1. Your classroom. Yes, I agree, it is a bit depressing at the moment but it has huge potential and our Interior Design expert, McCartney Stephens, has some wonderful ideas for making it Perfect.

2. The Dining Room. Well, I'm glad I sat and had my dinner with you guys. It *definitely* needs a makeover and that's what we'll do.

3. Dinners. You were right—the Savoy, it ain't! A little more inspiration is needed here so we'll be inviting a celebrity chef into school to assist Mrs Whitburn.

4. Teachers. Mmm . . . Mrs Mazurka, Mrs Ridley, and Mrs Towers would all benefit

from a makeover so our team will endeavour to make your teachers *Perfect*.

5. Playtimes and Assemblies. Our finale will reveal an instant improvement to these. More will be revealed as the week progresses.

We'll be arriving at school on Monday October 17th. However, there's just one more detail: Mrs Mazurka was under some pressure from the governors about *Perfect Schools*. They have asked that you, Paige, Shamir, and Finlay keep detailed diaries for the week so that it appears to have educational worth. I think that's a cool idea because KBC may be able to use them in a commercial sort-of spin off. You never know!

This is going to be so brilliant, Leanne.

Bye for now,

Evergreen.

'I'm not!' Finlay said, when I'd finished reading. He turned away from us and kicked at the pebbles, aiming one at the school fence.

'You're not *what*?' Paige questioned, placing her hands on her hips.

'Doing a diary. I'm useless at writing,' Finlay replied.

'Well, we have to do it, Finlay, whether you like it or not,' Paige said. 'It says it there in black and white.'

'I won't be in it then.'

'I'll help you, mate,' Shamir offered, pulling Finlay around.

'And me,' I said.

'Why should you help him?' Paige argued. 'You should do it yourself, Finlay.'

'Don't be so mean,' Shamir said. 'Finlay can't help the way he is.'

'I'm not being mean,' Paige responded. 'If you can't do something simple like write a diary, Finlay, you shouldn't be in it.'

'Hang on a minute, it don't actually say anything about *writing* a diary,' Shamir explained.

'What d'you mean?' Finlay asked, becoming interested again.

'You could keep a diary on a little tape recorder or a camcorder or something,' Shamir suggested.

'That's not fair,' Paige protested, folding her arms.

'Well, that's what Evergreen did,' Shamir remembered. 'She didn't write loads of notes about our school—she just took pictures and filmed us.'

'What a fantastic idea,' I said. 'My dad's got a brilliant little recorder that he uses at meetings. He won't miss it for a week.'

'And you just hand the tape in, Finlay, when we're finished,' Shamir said.

'But . . .' Paige pouted.

'Paige, you're *brilliant* at writing,' I said, 'so it's not like hard work for you, is it?'

'I suppose,' Paige agreed, smiling. It's easy to get round Paige, she simply needs flattering.

'We're all set!' I said. And when Mrs Mazurka wrote to our parents a few days later, we really were ready to become the Perfect School.

```
Venus Crescent Primary School
        Venus Crescent
       Universe Estate
          Leicester
```

October 10th

Dear Parents,

After many weeks of negotiations and careful preparation, I am happy to announce that the *PERFECT SCHOOLS* television crew will be in the school from October 17th for five days.

It is, of course, a great honour for the school and also a very exciting time for our children and teachers. We will do our very best to minimize any disruption to the normal timetable but there will have to be some minor changes. We apologize for any inconvenience there may be for the children or your good selves.

On Monday October 17th television cameras will be operating throughout the school, filming children primarily in the hall and the dining room. They will also be filming the renovation of Mrs Ridley's classroom.

On Tuesday October 18th: A renowned television makeover expert will be in school to present ideas and suggestions for brightening up the dining room. We would welcome any parents who would like to help with the work in this area of the school.

On Wednesday October 19th: A mystery celebrity chef (We are hoping for Jamie Oliver!) will work with some of the children and Mrs Whitburn at *enhancing* the lunchtime fare available. We will need some parent helpers in the kitchen on this day. If you are willing to assist us, please sign the slip below.

On Thursday October 20th: television psychologists and style experts will be on site to work with me and a small number of staff. In the words of the television company, 'A Perfect School needs Perfect Teachers!'

On Friday October 21st: In the morning, a television fitness guru will advise midday supervisors about aerobic activities for lunchtimes. Then, in the afternoon, the two main presenters of *PERFECT SCHOOLS* will be at Venus Crescent to film their parts. They will be working mainly with the team who have been chosen specially to help out with this project.

There may be an opportunity for all of us to see a finished video of the programme at a later date. In the meantime, I ask for your patience and co-operation as we prepare for this ground-breaking week in the history of our school.

Once again, we need your permission to film the children. Please sign the slip below and return to school by **October 14th.**

Yours faithfully,

(Mrs) Madeline Mazurka
Headteacher

I would like to help the Mystery Celebrity Chef in the kitchen on Wednesday October 19th.

Signed..

Parent/Guardian of...........................Class..........

I do/do not give permission for

Name ....Class...................

to be filmed by Kids Broadcasting Company.

Signed[Parent/Guardian].....................Date........

LEANNE'S DIARY: SUNDAY EVENING
OCTOBER 16TH

So, tomorrow, the *Perfect Schools* team arrives and I'm so excited. I don't think I'll be able to sleep tonight.

I called to my nan's after school last Monday to show her Mrs Mazurka's letter. Nan smiled as she read it. 'That's brilliant,' she said, in a really excited voice because she knew how much it meant to me. Then she read it again. 'Makes it sound as though *she's* done all the work,' Nan said, suspiciously.

'Who?'

'Mrs Mazurka—it says here, after weeks of negotiations and careful preparation, as if it was all her.'

'I know,' I agreed. 'She's a bit like that.'

'I just hope she doesn't take over after all your hard work, Leanne.'

'She won't, Nan,' I said confidently.

'Well, good luck to you, Leanne. I hope it'll be absolutely perfect!'

'So do I, Nan.'

It will be perfect and nobody's going to take over. This is going to be our week. We're going to transform our school into a Perfect School and nobody's going to stop us.

I just hope I can get to sleep.

12
Monday

'We would like a new classroom! It is the worst one in the world because it hasn't been painted for about a hundred years and we have to climb two sets of steep stone steps to reach it.'

'On Monday October 17th television cameras will be operating throughout the school, filming children primarily in the hall and the dining room. They will also be filming the renovation of Mrs Ridley's classroom.'

I hardly slept a wink all night, I was that excited. But I didn't feel at all tired when Paige called for me to walk to school. 'Notice anything different about me?' she asked.

I stopped and looked at her. 'No.'

'You'll have to be a bit more observant than that if you're going to be on the telly, Leanne.'

'Is it your hair, Paige?' I guessed.

'Yes! I had it done specially on Saturday,' Paige replied, excitedly.

'It looks lovely, Paige,' I said. 'I like those sort of blonde streaks, they really suit you and it's good the way it's been cut, too.'

'Thanks, Leanne. This is going to be so brilliant, isn't it?' We ran the rest of the way to school, and when we turned into Venus Crescent we stopped and stared for a few moments at the huge number of KBC vans parked all the way up the road outside school.

In the playground, faces were pressed against the fence, watching the television crew unload the equipment. Finlay shouted, 'Can I have your autograph, mister?' to one of the van drivers. He laughed.

Mrs Mazurka blew the whistle for the start of school. It took a few minutes for everyone to settle and listen. 'There's a slight change of plan this morning,' she shouted. 'I'd like you to file into school in your normal class groups, leave your coats and stuff in your rooms, and then come straight down to the hall for a special assembly. Mrs Marsh's class—lead on.'

Paige and I linked arms as we walked into school. 'This is going to be so excellent,' I said, excitedly. And it was. As we filed into the hall we could hear rap music playing and these dancers wearing purple and yellow gear encouraged us to start clapping to the music.

'Wow!' Paige said. 'This is so cool.'

'Much better than a normal Monday,' Finlay agreed.

'But it's so noisy,' Shamir complained.

'Oh wow, Leanne!' Paige shouted. 'Look who's at the front. I can't believe it.'

Paige and most of the kids in school were pointing at Heaven and Devon, the two main presenters of *Perfect Schools*, who had jumped onto the stage and were now dancing, wearing earpieces and clip-on microphones. They shouted, 'Yo, kids, get moving!' and waved back at the hundreds of hands pointing at them.

Then together they began:

'Step to the left and now to the right and
     . . . clap clap! clap clap!
Straight'n yer back till ya reach yer full
     height and . . . clap clap! clap, clap!
Listen to the music, dance to the beat and
     . . . clap clap! clap clap!
Get wav'n' yer arms and shuffl'n' yer feet
     and . . . clap clap! clap clap!
Do what we say, cos this is the rule and
     . . . clap clap! clap clap!
Cos we're gonna make you the cool-est
     school . . . **yeeaahhh!**'

We all cheered and whistled and jumped about. Cameras in every corner zoomed in and out filming us. When Evergreen and Mrs Mazurka walked onto the stage, everyone went wild with excitement, clapping, cheering and whistling again. Heaven called out, 'Girls and boys, welcome . . . Mrs Mazurka!' and we all went mad again. I don't know why but I think we would have cheered if a crying baby had crawled across the stage.

Then Devon said, 'OK, let's say a big hello

to . . . Evergreen!' Devon waited a bit and then added, 'Now, Evergreen's the cool chick who's going to knock you into shape this week, ain't you, Evergreen?'

'Yeah. What have you lot had for breakfast?' Evergreen cried and four hundred voices replied, 'Bacon butty! Cornflakes! Sausages! Crisps! Nothing! Eggs! Chocolate! Weetabix!'

'OK, OK,' Evergreen shouted. 'Now it's time to settle down and chill out and *listen*. Some of you already know me but for those who don't, I'm Evergreen, and along with my team and your help, we're going to transform Venus Crescent Primary into a Perfect School, yeah!' And we all started clapping and screaming and shouting again. 'So I want my team to come up here, please. Girls and boys, say a big hello to . . . Finlay! Shamir! Paige and . . . the person who has made all this happen . . . Leanne!' The moment my name was mentioned the whistling and cheering was louder than ever. I felt like I'd won *Pop Idol* or something.

What a fantastic start to the week! This was better than I had ever expected. Mrs Mazurka cleared her throat, waited for silence and talked for a few minutes about best behaviour and visitors and then Evergreen asked us to act naturally and not to take any notice of the cameras around school. As if! Then we left the hall to music, dancing, and clapping and danced along the corridor and up the stairs to our classroom. As we reached the top of the stairs, Mrs Ridley turned to look at us with a face like a thundery sky.

Ah well, I thought, *we're not perfect yet.*

Paige's Diary

I've got this massive feeling that this week is going to change my life for ever. Mum wants me to really shine out for the telly so we went to the hairdresser's on Saturday and I had these sort of, like, low-lights put in my hair. They kind of bring out the blonde which was fading because it just does as you grow. My mum says that when I was a toddler my hair was pure white and even

strangers used to stop her and say, hasn't
your baby got gorgeous hair.

It was brilliant when we started on this
project because when I grow up I would
like to be something like a model or an
actress or a singer-songwriter and you have
to be sort of noticed by people to get
famous. Another thing I know is you have
to be prepared to work really hard doing
jobs you don't like. Now I'm not keen on
moving furniture but when we took all the
tables and chairs from our room down to
the hall, I smiled and pretended I was
enjoying myself although Evergreen said not
to smile too much. We had to show that
it was an effort.

There was loads of cameramen and
women in our room. When we'd finished our
removal job, Evergreen showed us how they'd
speeded up the film so it looked like it only
took us a few seconds to clear the room.
Leanne says they do that a lot on home

improvement shows. Makes people think everything's dead easy.

Just then McCartney Stephens, the celebrity Interior Designer, arrived with Mrs Mazurka behind him, twittering and giggling like a star-struck teenager all the way up the stairs. I'm not surprised, because he is extremely famous. Leanne almost fainted when he appeared. I was perfectly cool and calm, as a true professional should be.

McCartney walked into the classroom, shook hands with each of us and then swirled around like a ballroom dancer doing a solo routine. 'Wow!' he cried. 'This is magnificent.' He had a black leather satchel which he placed, very dramatically, in the centre of the empty classroom.

'Right,' Mrs Mazurka said, in a really high-pitched voice. 'Well, I'll get back to my office if you don't need me.'

'You carry on, Madeline,' McCartney said soothingly and he blew her a kiss.

Finlay and Shamir giggled like toddlers who've been tickled. Honestly! I wish those boys would be a bit more mature, especially in front of the media.

'OK, kids,' Evergreen began, 'I want to see real surprise and joy and delight on your faces at how your classroom is going to be transformed. OK?'

'Yes!' I replied, enthusiastically.

'If anything, I'd like you to overdo your expressions. There's no such thing as under-statement on KBC, OK?' I understood what Evergreen meant, so did Leanne, though I could tell that Shamir and Finlay were confused, to say the least.

McCartney lifted a laptop computer from his bag and the cameras zoomed in on it, briefly. 'My vision of how this room will look,' McCartney began, tapping keys on the laptop, 'is of a room swathed in light and bright colours. These large beams have to go, of course.'

'You can't do that,' Finlay protested. 'The roof will cave in.' See what I mean? The boy's a huge embarrassment.

'Quite right!' McCartney agreed. 'So we have to *disguise* them.'

'How d'you do that?' Shamir asked.

'Moustache, dark glasses, and a wig?' Finlay suggested. I cringed but I tried not to show it.

'And a long coat with a turned-up collar,' Shamir added, laughing. I gave Shamir one of my withering looks.

'Like it, like it!' Evergreen said, smiling. Strange.

McCartney smiled too. 'No, I suggest we sand these beams and then paint them a kind of wheaten colour (At this point Finlay muttered 'What, like bread?' but everyone ignored him, thank goodness.) with the same for the walls so they kind of blend in. Then . . .' he tapped another key on the laptop, 'I want us to think of this room in the roof as a kind of loft apartment so I'd like to make a lounge area . . .' Click.

'That's well cool,' I said, staring at the computer screen. 'I love those red sofas and that low coffee table—it's like something out of IKEA.'

'Next,' click, 'we're going to have a work area.'

Leanne said, 'Wow! I like the way you've got those big plants in-between the tables.'

'Yes, I thought of it like an open-plan office kind of thing where you're sort of working together but you won't . . . distract one another,' McCartney said. 'So, what do you think, kids?'

I swung my hair back and smiled straight at a camera. 'Well, I think it's fantastic,' I said.

Evergreen put her thumbs up at me and sort of pointed at Finlay and Shamir to get them to say something. Finlay said, 'I like it all right but where will everyone fit?'

'They'll fit,' McCartney replied.

'I can't wait to get going,' Leanne said.

'Right!' McCartney said, rubbing his hands together. 'So . . . let's go!'

Finlay

Taping, taping, one, two, three. I like this tape recorder Leanne brought in for me, it's really dinky.

In the afternoon, Evergreen gave us purple and yellow overalls and huge pieces of sandpaper and showed us how to rub the beams to prepare them for painting. As soon as we started doing the hard graft Paige began complaining. She's such a . . . girlie. First it was, this will ruin my nails, so Evergreen gave her some purple rubber gloves and then it was, what about my hair? So Evergreen gave her a yellow hair net. She looked well stupid and me and Shamir couldn't stop giggling every time we looked at her. Leanne told us to pack it in and get on with it. Shamir said this is the best thing we've ever done in school. He's right—it's a wicked laugh.

My hands are a bit sore after the sanding . . . but we only did it by ourselves for a few minutes and then a few telly assistants helped, cos they want to get our room done in a day and they need about twenty seconds of film of us doing the work. This is better than doing sums or literacy because I can like . . . do it.

It was well wicked when we started painting. Paige was dripping paint all over, Shamir hardly put any paint on his brush, like he was a bit scared of it, and Leanne worked like a real painter and decorator. Mac stood in the corner making notes on his palm pilot. Said he couldn't help cos he'd got his best clothes on and, he says, designers don't do heavy work. I'll have to remember that excuse.

LEANNE: MONDAY EVENING

This has been the very best day of my life. We've finished our classroom and it looks fabulous! The classroom of my dreams. As soon as the painting was finished, all the settees and plants and everything were brought in and Mac showed where they should be placed.

So this is how it looks now: you walk in the door and on the left-hand side there's the lounge area with three sofa units which link together around the coffee table. They all face the Wide Screen Telly with DVD and entertainment system.

On the other side of the room there's the work area and all these lovely, leafy plants separating the tables. They're like a portable hedge.

It is the classroom of my dreams. I am so happy.

Tomorrow we are going to transform the dining room with another very famous person. I can't wait.

13

Tuesday

'Will you do something about our dining room? It's a total and utter disgrace and even if we did have tasty and non-toxic food, the state of the dining room puts you off eating.'

'On Tuesday October 18th: A renowned television makeover expert will be in school to present ideas and suggestions for brightening up the dining room. We would welcome any parents who would like to help with the work in this area of the school.'

I actually ate some breakfast this morning and then I ran to school, I was that excited. Evergreen gathered us four together in the playground before school. 'We're going to make a start on the dining room immediately,' Evergreen said. 'So let's go.'

The cameras were already there. 'Morning!' Finlay shouted and then him and Shamir started doing high fives with the crew. Mrs Whitburn stood behind the counter, arms folded, scowling at us.

Evergreen read her notes for a few minutes and scratched her head until she looked up suddenly and said, 'How about this: you talk to me about the state of the dining hall. Tell me how it depresses you when you're eating and puts you off your food and so on and so on.'

We sat and stared at one another in silence. I didn't really understand what we were supposed to do so I waited for someone else to start. But nobody did. 'Not good television!' Evergreen announced from behind the cameras. 'Definitely *not* KBC! Just start . . . talking,' she urged us.

'What about?' I asked. 'I don't really get what you're on about.'

'Neither do I,' Paige said.

Finlay and Shamir were waving at kids who'd gathered outside the window. 'Get rid of them, somebody,' Evergreen directed. She walked noisily over to us and knelt down next to the table. 'This is what I suggest: Leanne, you start off by talking to your mates as though we're not here and you say something like, oh, I don't know . . .' She twitched about a bit as she thought. 'Say . . . this room is *so* uncool or something and then Finlay say something like, yeah, it puts me off my dinner . . . and the rest of you chip in. OK?'

'I understand now,' Paige said, brightly.

'But just relax—yeah? Be yourselves,' Evergreen said, encouragingly. She walked over behind the camera and put her thumbs up as we started again.

'I hate eating my dinner in this room,' I said.

'Me too,' Paige agreed.

'And me,' Finlay said.

'Same here,' Shamir added. Then we all giggled.

'OK, wait,' Evergreen called. She walked over to our table and knelt down next to us again.

'I thought that was brilliant. A fantastic start but . . . instead of just agreeing, Paige, can you say something like . . . oh, I don't know . . . say . . . it's so depressing and then Finlay you say something like . . . wouldn't it be so cool if we could decorate it and Shamir, you say something like . . .' Evergreen scratched her head as she thought. '. . . oh, I don't know— dinner times would be better or—get the idea?'

'I know what you mean,' Paige said. Finlay and Shamir still looked puzzled.

'Right—we'll start again,' Evergreen sighed and walked back behind the camera.

'I hate eating my dinner in this room,' I repeated.

'So do I,' Paige agreed. 'It's depressing!' She slumped forward in a dramatic way and rested her head on her arm. Evergreen put her thumbs up again.

'Wouldn't it be so . . . cool,' Finlay said as if he was reading from a script, 'if we could do this room up and . . .'

'Dinner times would be much better,' Shamir said in an unusual, high-pitched voice.

I could tell that Evergreen wasn't all that pleased. She put her hands on her head and paced around the edge of the room, occasionally breaking off to stare at us. 'I know what's missing!' she cried, clicking her fingers. 'Food! We need to do it all again but you need food on the table . . .'

'Great idea, Evergreen,' Paige agreed. 'And we can be poking about with our food as we talk. You know, as if it's really disgusting and the state of the room is really, really putting us off our food.'

Evergreen said, 'Wonderful, Paige!'

Paige looked triumphant.

Shamir

It takes ages for Mrs Whitburn to rustle up a few miserable salads and then she throws them in front of us and scurries back to the kitchen. We film that bit and it goes OK.

Then Evergreen asks us for any ideas for the dining room and I says, yes: it's to do with our school being called Venus Crescent and us being on the Universe Estate and all that . . . and my mate Finlay says, tell them about the muriel you was thinking of, Shamir. Evergreen says, do you mean mural?

Yeah—sort of, I says. Why don't we do something on the planets, you know, the solar system? Finlay says, that's a well cool idea and Leanne says, that's a brilliant idea, Shamir, we could do a kind of blue background on one wall . . .

Even Paige got into it (she normally hates anything boys suggest). Why don't we paint the ceiling navy blue as if it's the night? she says, dead excited and all. So I says, what d'you think, Evergreen? But I can already tell from her face what she's thinking.

My mate Finlay says, tell us the rest, so I says, we can use silver and luminous paint and all sorts. Evergreen says, tell you what, let's see what our makeover expert thinks, shall we? Is it McCartney Stephens in his best clothes again? Finlay asks and Evergreen says no, it's somebody new and just then he walks in.

Falcon Thompson! Paige says. From that *Sweeping Brooms* programme.

Yeah! he says.

Nice jacket, mate, Finlay says.

Good taste, pal! Falcon replies, all chummy, pointing at Finlay.

My nan loves your programme, Leanne says.

Well, she's one cool chick, your nan, Falcon replies and we all laugh cos Leanne's nan's ancient. She's about fifty!

He shakes hands with all of us, unzips a large, flat briefcase and says, Got any ideas about what you want to do, kids?

The kids have some really cool ideas, Evergreen says, but they're dying to hear what you're going to say. Are we?

He pulls this huge sheet of paper out of the bag. Evergreen, he says—wonderful photos and video! I had a long look at them and I thought we could start off with a pastelly pink sort of background in this room.

That's a bit girly, Finlay says.

Not any more! Falcon replies. Pastelly pink is *so* in. And men have reclaimed pink. It is no longer . . . *girly*.

Definitely, Evergreen nods her head.

And on top of that pastelly pink background

we could do some huge wavy stripes of lilac and purple and indigo . . . he says.

I'm thinking—*is he for real?* so I says, what about the planets?

That's Shamir's idea, Evergreen explains.

Yeah, we could work the planets into it, in an abstract sort of way, I suppose, Falcon says but he's sort of squirming.

Out the corner of my eye I see Leanne getting all sort of rumbly, so she asks, What about Shamir's ideas? It's supposed to be . . .

Leanne, darling, Evergreen says, but she don't mean darling, We have the best designer in the business here, at great expense to the programme so I think that we should let him get on with it. And she clips her words dead short like she's well annoyed.

I'll do my best to incorporate whatever you suggest, Falcon says. Tell you what, we can have pink planets! What d'you think of that, mate?

I'll be honest, I'm well crushed. I slouch in my chair and fold my arms and I'm thinking, are you serious. Then I'm thinking, it's supposed to be *our* ideas. But I don't say nothing.

I know Shamir was disappointed but it was still a really brilliant day. Falcon Thompson tried to explain to Shamir that in television, you have to let the experts make the decisions, otherwise it would be a disaster. Paige said, 'But on *Sweeping Brooms*, the owners have all the ideas and do all the work.'

'That's how it *appears*,' Falcon said, smiling cheekily; and then he started work, measuring out the walls and that. Every few minutes parents and teachers kept coming in and asking for his autograph or saying, 'Do you need any help?'

'Yes,' he kept saying, 'many hands . . .' So the dining room became quite crowded and Mrs Whitburn's scowl was growing deeper. Most of the mums giggled as Falcon Thompson stood next to them for photos.

'He's the absolute Alan Titchmarsh of makeovers,' one of the mums said.

I would like to say that it's my dream

dining room, but it isn't, because I do feel disappointed for Shamir. It's still brilliant, though. We need to get the dinners sorted now. That's tomorrow.

I really, really hope that the celebrity chef is Jamie Oliver. Fingers crossed.

14

Wednesday

'We would like a new cook! Most of the kids in this school are hungry every afternoon because they know that the cook is trying to poison us with her recipes. Honestly, Evergreen, the food is pure disgusting.'

'On Wednesday October 19th: A mystery celebrity chef (We are hoping for Jamie Oliver!) will work with some of the children and Mrs Whitburn at *enhancing* the lunchtime fare available. There may be a *few* spaces for parents to attend this event.'

On Wednesday morning my mouth was watering at the thought of some decent food for school dinner. We were all anxiously awaiting the arrival of Jamie Oliver because I was sure it would be him but he still hadn't arrived at eleven o'clock. Mrs Whitburn was bursting with anger and anxiety. 'I've got three hundred kiddies to cook for! What am I supposed to do?' she raged. Me and Paige, Finlay and Shamir were standing at the back of the dining room watching and waiting. 'Specially after that fiasco yesterday,' Mrs Whitburn continued. 'What with those kiddies eating their dinners with that terrible smell of paint.'

'Darling, calm down. Television is not an exact science,' Evergreen said. 'We have timetables and schedules, yes . . . but stars aren't paid to arrive on time . . . and as for the painting . . .'

'What about today's dinner?' Mrs Whitburn interrupted, impatiently. 'What are we going to do for today?'

'Look—don't worry about dinner,' Evergreen said, brightly. 'We'll just have it a bit later today, the kids won't mind. It's a great adventure for them.'

Then the celebrity chef arrived and it wasn't Jamie Oliver. It was Jimmy D'Ollio. He swept into the room with a crowd of assistants and shouted, 'Evergreen, you got any 'eadache pills? I've got a massive 'angover.'

'Jimmy, darling!' Evergreen shouted, rushing over to greet him.

'Jimmy *D'Ollio*, you mean!' he replied, smiling, and he hugged Evergreen and gave her two pretend kisses on the cheek.

'Yuck!' Finlay whispered.

'Pass the bucket,' Shamir added, pretending to be sick.

'Stoppit, you two, don't be so immature,' Paige hissed. 'That's just what telly people are like.'

'Look at Mrs Whitburn,' I whispered.

'Yeah—she don't look angry any more, does she?' Finlay said. 'Look at her, smoothing her hair back and smiling like a blooming film star!'

Evergreen produced a packet of tablets and a glass of water and handed them quietly to Jimmy. 'These'll make you feel heaps better.'

'Any gin in this?' Jimmy asked and then he chuckled.

'Doesn't he know that this is a school not a pub,' Paige muttered.

'Chill out, Paige,' Finlay hissed.

We watched him carefully as he drank. 'Have you ever seen him or heard of him before?' Shamir asked. Paige gave him one of her withering looks.

'He's on telly in the day,' I replied. 'I saw him the other week when I was off with that stomach bug. He's brilliant. He's dead funny.'

Paige's Diary

Mrs Whitburn walked over to meet Jimmy and sort of curtsied. (Daft woman!) 'I watch all your programmes, Jimmy,' she said, hesitatingly.

'She must tape them,' Leanne whispered.

'You got a telly in your kitchen then, girl?' Jimmy asked. We all giggled.

'I tape them,' Mrs Whitburn said, winking at Jimmy. 'You're an inspiration.'

'Risotto!' Jimmy said, clapping his hands together.

'That's his word for brilliant,' Leanne explained.

'OK, so . . . I've been thinking about our menu for today, Mrs W, and I thought . . . how about fragrant Mediterranean meat balls in a chilli sauce with rice and vegetables and for the veggies: baked eggs served on a bed of parsnip and parsley mash. Very now! Extremely risotto! Puddings . . . how about . . . caramelized rhubarb, with a titchy bit of crème fraiche. What says you about that, Mrs W, my old pal?'

Mrs Whitburn looked around at the cameras and crew. She hadn't a clue what to say. Evergreen called across, 'Say something!'

Mrs Whitburn took a deep breath. 'We'll need a bigger chalkboard.'

'Is that all you can say, Mrs W?' Jimmy asked, grinning. 'You're a card and no mistake.'

'Mrs Whitburn, we need you to say something about the actual food,' Evergreen reminded her.

'I don't think our kids will eat this,' Mrs Whitburn began. 'They're very fussy and they seem to like plain stuff, Jamie.'

'Jimmy!' Jimmy corrected her, placing his hand on his forehead. 'Yeah, but don't you think we need to spice up their lives a bit?'

'It's just—I know our kids. They don't like nothing new . . .'

'Cut!' Evergreen shouted. 'Mrs Whitburn, you're supposed to say, that would be wonderful, Jimmy, let's give it a go or something like that.'

'But what if I already know that they . . .'

'This is *television*,' Evergreen said. 'Not a meeting of your kitchen staff. Just agree with Jimmy so that we can actually get on with the cooking.'

We all looked at one another as we watched from the back of the dining room. For once, Mrs Whitburn was right. Kids wouldn't eat what Jimmy was suggesting. But that didn't seem to matter.

Then I started thinking, Why isn't he talking to *us* about what *we* like to eat?

Finlay's Diary

Taping, taping, one, two, three . . . I think I might ask my mum if I can have a tape recorder like this.

Jimmy D'Ollio looked a right wreck but Leanne said he's meant to, that's why people like him. Anyway, after Mrs Whitburn were sorted we got called to the kitchen. Evergreen dressed us in cooks' gear. I felt well stupid. But then Jimmy came over and he was doing high fives and acting all laddish and going, 'You look absolutely risotto,' and all that. He even made Paige smile.

Bit of a shock when we pushed open the kitchen door, ready to start—the place was stuffed with women in white coats and starched hats. Normally, there are only about five kitchen staff but I could see at least fifty women, including my mum (oh, well shown-up!), Shamir's mum, Mrs Mazurka, and almost all the teachers, apart from Mrs Ridley. Honest, I'm not kidding, they looked like blooming battery hens.

Jimmy backed out of the kitchen. 'Mrs W,' he called. 'Like . . . what is happening here?'

'Well, some are my staff,' Mrs Whitburn said, 'And some are on work experience and we often have a number of volunteers in the kitchen and some are specially invited guests.'

'Work experience?' Jimmy questioned. 'Volunteers? Guests?'

'Yes,' Mrs Whitburn said, nodding her head. Jimmy just stared at her.

Then Mrs Mazurka stepped forward looking well ridiculous in a cook's outfit. 'I'm the headteacher, so I'll explain, Jimmy,' Mrs Mazurka began. 'I'm so delighted to meet you— I watch all of your programmes and I'm a very hands-on head and I encourage my staff to be similarly active in all parts of the school so— most of my teachers are here this morning to witness your master class.'

'And get on the telly,' I whispered to my mate, Shamir.

'What about the kids?' Jimmy asked. 'Who's teaching them?'

'They're on an extended break being supervised by Mrs Towers, our very able midday supervisor-co-ordinator.'

I tried to keep quiet but I couldn't help it. Neither could Shamir. We just laughed so loud until Paige gave us one of her looks. I could tell that Leanne was dying to laugh, too.

Jimmy was not well pleased. 'Evergreen!' he called. 'I cannot work . . . like this. It is not a risotto situation for me.'

'I know it's gonna be hard, Jimmy, especially with your headache but can you . . . I don't know, ignore all that's going on around you and . . . just carry on as if they're not here?' Evergreen suggested.

'Can't you, like . . . get rid of them?' Jimmy whispered.

'Well . . . no,' Evergreen said.

'I ain't never known nothing like this before,' Jimmy said.

'That's because we're a *unique* school, Jamie,' Mrs Mazurka said, smiling.

'Jimmy!' he shouted. Then he straightened his shoulders as if he was going into battle 'Right! Let's go?' The women started clapping. Jimmy glared at them. 'I don't want to hear nothing! Got it, you lot?'

'Right, OK, fine,' everyone muttered.

'First of all we'll start with the veggie dish cos my mate Shamir tells me there ain't no cool veggie cooking here. 'S'at right, Shamir?'

Shamir glanced uneasily towards Mrs Whitburn. 'Sometimes,' he said quietly.

'Hasn't he told you about my Cheese Surprise?' Mrs Whitburn asked. Jimmy said nothing.

'So . . . are you watching? Kids—you'll need to lean forward,' Jimmy said. As he did, the women also shoved forward to get a better view. Jimmy was pressed against the preparation bench. 'Get off!' he yelled.

'I can't see a thing,' a voice called out from the back. Sounded like my mum. Well embarrassing!

'Mind my foot!' another yelled.

'Who do you think you're pushing!'

'You'd better watch out for my varicose veins!'

'Manners!'

Jimmy's voice rose above the commotion. 'First of all, we're going to peel the potatoes and parsnips. Are you watching? This is my absolute risotto method for peeling vegetables. So if you're gonna do it right, you gotta use a Jimmy D'Ollio vegetable peeler . . .'

Just then I noticed the commotion outside the kitchen windows. I nudged Shamir. Children were running wild. Mrs Towers was chasing after them and yelling, 'Go and stand next to the fence, this minute!'

Kids were banging on the windows shouting, 'Mum!' when they spotted their mothers desperately trying to watch Jimmy peel vegetables. Even Mrs Mazurka never noticed the riot outside.

It didn't seem real. Kids from all classes charging around outside the school, totally ignoring Mrs Towers while teachers and parents and Mrs Mazurka were crammed into the school kitchen, watching Jimmy D'Ollio showing them how to *peel potatoes*.

The place had gone mad. Totally mad.

LEANNE: WEDNESDAY EVENING

We had sandwiches for dinner today. They were lovely, much better than normal dinners. Finlay's mum started making them at about one o'clock right at the back of the kitchen, away from the crowds and the cameras.

Jimmy D'Ollio's meal was ready at about a quarter to three, then—this is the worst bit—me, Paige, Finlay, and Shamir had to taste it and pretend we were enjoying eating it. Jimmy was hopping about next to us going, 'Ain't it the most risotto meal you've ever tasted, kids?'

Shamir said, 'No,' dead quietly.

Evergreen said, 'Bright smiles, positive comments, and then we can wrap this up for today.' But it was hard because the food tasted totally disgusting.

That made me feel a bit cheated because Jimmy D'Ollio hadn't improved Mrs Whitburn's cooking at all. He gave her a signed copy of his latest cookbook and said, 'You stick to that, Mrs W, and you'll be cooking the most risotto meals every day.' I could tell from the look on her face that Jimmy's book would never be opened again.

Tomorrow, Mrs Ridley and Mrs Mazurka will be made-over and talked to by a famous psychologist.

That should be interesting.

15

Thursday

'We would like new teachers! Mrs Ridley, our class teacher, is the grumpiest grunt in the whole of civilization. We want someone who likes a bit of fun and who . . . smiles. It's not too much to ask, is it? While you're at it, you could get rid of Mrs Mazurka too. She's not old but she's become very bo-ring and she gives us long dreary lectures in assembly.'

'On Thursday October 20th: television psychologists and style experts will be on site to work with me and a small number of adult staff. In the words of the television company, "A Perfect School needs Perfect Teachers!"'

On Thursday morning I noticed a stranger standing at the corner of the playground. He was making notes on a clipboard and watching as the children ran around. (Not too wildly, because there isn't enough space, so Mrs Mazurka said.) Evergreen was hovering next to him. Kids kept darting behind him and trying to see what he was writing. He smiled at them and held his notes close to his chest.

'Who's he then?' Finlay asked as we walked over towards Evergreen.

'He's called Devalera Duffy and he's the presenter of that programme, *Behaving Madly*,' Paige explained. 'My mum loves it.'

'Your mum watches loads of telly,' Shamir observed.

'So? What's wrong with that, Shamir?'

'Nothing,' Shamir replied.

'You can learn a lot from the telly, you know,' Paige continued. 'He does another programme, too, called *How Not to Behave*.'

'What's that about?' Finlay asked.

'Don't you watch anything?' Paige questioned.

'He only watches Postman Pat videos,' Shamir

answered, laughing. Then him and Finlay started wrestling.

'Boys!' Paige tutted. 'Let's go over and talk to him, Leanne.' She pulled at my sleeve as she started to weave her way through the other children in the playground.

Devalera Duffy smiled brightly as Evergreen introduced us. He had a similar Irish accent to my nan. 'You're a great girl, Leanne,' he said, as he shook hands with me. (That's the sort of thing my nan says all the time.) 'Getting all this going. I can't wait to meet your teachers after all I've heard about them.'

'My mum loves your programmes,' Paige said.

'Does she? What's her favourite?'

'She likes *Behaving Madly*. She says she can't believe some of the stupid things that people do . . .'

'I know. It's an absolute gas doing that programme,' Devalera replied.

'OK, Dev,' Evergreen interrupted. 'The crew are waiting for you in the beautifully refurbished dining room, so . . . if you'll follow me

I'll introduce you to your clients for today; and, kids . . . I'll meet you in your superb new classroom at playtime!'

Mrs Marsh blew the whistle for the start of school so we lined up in our class groups and filed into the building. In the hall, where we were having our lessons, we met our supply teacher for the day, Miss Redbridge. Her grey hair was scraped back harshly from her face into a tight bun and she spoke in a stern, boring monotone. Suddenly, Mrs Ridley didn't seem too bad.

It seemed like an age until playtime when Paige, Shamir, Finlay, and I climbed the stairs to our new classroom and waited for Evergreen.

Shamir

Me, Leanne, Paige, and my mate Finlay, we was sitting on the red sofas in our new classroom, all casual and relaxed and Evergreen says, now, we've got the best in the business here today to make your teachers look better. You tell us what you want us to do.

So Paige starts off, as she would cos she

reckons she's a fashion expert. Mrs Mazurka's hair is too short for her face, she says, and I don't like those posh suits she wears. They don't suit her.

Yeah, Leanne agrees, and Mrs Ridley needs to be taught to smile. And her clothes are really old and dull.

Are you seriously going to put this on telly? Finlay asks, a bit nervous like. He pulls a leaf off the big plant next to the settee and starts rolling it up and fidgeting with it. Cos I think old Mrs Towers buys all her stuff from the Oxfam bargain rail but I wouldn't like to say it on the telly or she might make me stand next to the fence for the rest of my life.

Evergreen laughs. We'll only use a few seconds, she says, and it won't sound as if you're being nasty or anything.

Then we go back down to the hall and listen to Miss Redbridge, the supply teacher standing in for Mrs Ridley, who has a voice like a railway engine, it's so boring. She makes Mrs Ridley seem interesting. Anyway, I pretends to do my work and count the minutes. It takes hours.

Paige

Ten minutes before the end of the morning, Evergreen called for us and led us down to the dining room where Mrs Whitburn was standing with her arms folded angrily watching the cameras. The rest of the normal kitchen staff were banging about, getting ready for today's dinner. It seemed quite empty after yesterday. I could still smell the strong spices from Jimmy D'Ollio's cooking yesterday. It made me feel sick, like tasting the food all over again.

Evergreen let us stay for a few minutes to watch Annette Kirtan at work. She has a TV programme called *Nette's Notes* where she gives people £500 to spend and then helps them to choose the right outfits. She was sitting with Mrs Ridley, Mrs Mazurka, and Mrs Towers showing them catalogues and little bits of cloth before their trip into town to choose some new outfits.

I felt really, really jealous. Leanne said that we were going to be made into the perfect school and a school's about the kids as well but as this week has gone on, me and Leanne and Finlay and Shamir, we seem to be pushed more and more into the pink background of the new dining room.

LEANNE: THURSDAY EVENING

Our classroom wasn't ready until today, even though it seemed to be finished on Monday. There were lots of little jobs that needed finishing but they won't show any of that in the final version on telly.

They filmed us going back into our classroom, all of us. Everyone was going, 'Wow! This is fantastic!' and fighting over the spaces on the red settees. Evergreen shouted, 'Get off, you little brats, sit properly in your places.'

Shamir said, 'I knew this would happen. My mate Finlay said, remember, where's everyone going to sit?'

Finlay switched on the wide-screen telly and said, 'Anyone want to watch the racing?'

It was pandemonium. Evergreen kept clapping her hands and shouting, screeching, begging for us to calm down and sit down. Eventually, Shamir did a two-finger whistle and people started to listen.

'Find a place!' she commanded. 'Not in the lounge area. Now, sit down and be quiet until Mrs Ridley returns.'

Then five minutes before the bell, Mrs Ridley crept back into the room, followed by a camera crew. She was wearing a lilac trouser suit, a new hairstyle, and a smile, the first we had ever seen. 'You look wonderful, dear,' Evergreen remarked.

'Thanks,' Mrs Ridley whispered. 'I'll take over now.' She smiled at us. It was strange, very strange.

'I think she's been brainwashed,' Shamir hissed.

'I heard that,' Mrs Ridley said, still smiling. 'And the truth is, Shamir, my friend: I haven't been brainwashed. No, today I have got in touch with who I really am. And you know what?'

Thankfully, at that moment, the bell rang and we all breathed a huge sigh of relief. Mrs Ridley didn't rush from the room as she normally did. She smiled at us and continued, 'I just want you to know, you are great kids and I love and appreciate every single one of you.'

We rushed from the room. 'What's going on?' Shamir questioned as we raced down the stairs.

'She's finally flipped,' Finlay said.

I know that I said I wanted new teachers but this was a bit . . . weird.

Still, we've got Friday to look forward to. I wonder what they'll do?

16

Friday

'We would like a bigger playground where we can run around and have proper games without being told off and better assemblies with cool music and also chairs for the Year 6 kids to sit on so that when we go into assembly we don't have to be all squashed up.'

'On Friday October 21st: In the morning, a television fitness guru will advise lunchtime supervisors about aerobic activities for lunchtimes. Then, in the afternoon, the two main presenters of *PERFECT SCHOOLS* will be at Venus Crescent to film their parts. They will be working mainly with the team who have been chosen specially to help out with this project.'

For some reason, I didn't feel at all excited on Friday morning. I felt weary and sort of . . . flat. It wasn't just that our adventure was coming to an end. No, things hadn't gone the way I wanted them to. Paige felt the same. 'And I never thought I'd say this, Leanne, but I'm quite looking forward to having Mrs Ridley back, aren't you?'

'Yes. That Miss Redbridge was awful,' I agreed.

'And didn't Mrs Ridley look . . . different, yesterday, Leanne?'

'Yes, I thought she looked quite nice actually, Paige.'

We had to endure Mrs Redbridge again for the first hour on Friday morning while Mrs Mazurka and Mrs Ridley were re-filming some parts of their makeover. It was a very long, boring hour.

After playtime, Mrs Ridley was waiting for us in our classroom, wearing a sort of turquoise kaftan with matching trousers that really brought out the colour in her eyes. When everyone was back in the room, muttering and chattering about the new decor and furniture, Mrs Ridley asked us to sit on the floor. 'It's so hard to see you all behind those big plants.' Speaking in a low, quiet voice she continued, 'Children, I would like to share something with you.'

Finlay, who thought we were going to have a treat, said, 'Brilliant, sweeties!'

Mrs Ridley wasn't cross. She looked at Finlay kindly and said, 'Not that kind of sharing, Finlay.' Then she smiled, which was a rare thing for her. (Remember what I said about Mrs Ridley's smiles and bank holidays?) 'No, I want to share something very personal because I realize that I've been a bit of a grouch since the beginning of this term. Well, if I'm honest I haven't been happy for a long time and I feel that I ought to explain why.' She took a massive breath. Everyone was totally silent and still. Even Finlay had stopped fidgeting and shuffling. Then Mrs Ridley said, 'You see, things have been a bit difficult for me because—'

'OK, Leanne and gang!' Evergreen said,

bursting into the room. Mrs Ridley looked dead embarrassed as if someone had caught her on the toilet. She went bright red and looked as if she might cry. 'We need Leanne, Finlay, Shamir, and Paige in the hall because,' Evergreen stopped like a dancer before a difficult manoeuvre, held her arms out and announced, 'Gazelle is here!'

'Gazelle Smythe?' Paige asked, amazed.

'Yes!' Evergreen replied, triumphantly.

Paige

My mum absolutely *loves* Gazelle Smythe. She does all her exercises.

On the way down to the hall, Mrs Mazurka appeared from her office dressed in a skinny green T-shirt and matching combat trousers. She shook Gazelle's hand and gushed on about what a wonderful privilege it was to have her in the school and how much she enjoyed her programme—which is on at ten o'clock in the morning. Makes you wonder, doesn't it?

Shamir whispered, 'That's probably why she's always so behind with her work if she watches daytime TV.' And Leanne nodded her head, agreeing with him.

Me, Leanne, Finlay, and Shamir followed Mrs Mazurka, Evergreen, and Gazelle over to the hall. Mrs Mazurka flung open the doors in a really dramatic gesture. It looked brilliant. There was a new shiny wooden floor that was totally smooth and even. They must have fitted it during Thursday night. My mum says it's amazing what people can do if they put their minds to it.

Finlay

Taping, taping, one, two, three. I'm really getting the hang of this taping now.

'Wow!' Shamir shouted when we arrived at the hall. 'This is totally mega! What are we going to do?'

'Roller skating!' Evergreen yelled, dead natural.

'It's our alternative to boring assemblies and one way of coping with a small playground.' Assemblies? I didn't get what she was on about and by the look on Shamir's face, neither did he.

Gazelle Smythe was all smiling sweetly for the camera. 'What do you think of it, kids?' But us four were all a bit, like, gobsmacked and we just sort of stared at her.

Next thing you know, Evergreen pulled a trolley into the hall and over to Gazelle and she said, 'Roller skates!' like some people say, 'Dinner!' Mrs Mazurka and some of the mums waiting outside the hall ran in and pounced on the skate trolley like blooming vultures. So much for their manners.

My mum was there—well shown-up, again. Everyone was getting dead noisy with excitement, trying on different skates and saying things like, 'These don't fit,' and 'There's hardly any in big sizes!'

'Hang on!' Evergreen said. 'These are for the kids!' So the mums hung back a bit and let us four get our skates on first.

Me and my mate Shamir got our skates on and stumbled around for a bit trying to get our balance. I felt well stupid. Paige and Leanne was just a bit better. Then all the parents started kitting themselves out with skates and stuff. Mrs Towers and Old Madeline Mazurka pushed past me to reach the trolley. I almost went flying but Shamir got me just in time.

Next thing you know, Gazelle glides over to the edge of the hall and places one of them, like, radio microphones round her head. 'OK, kids,' she crackled. 'We need to get started so . . . find yourselves a space.' The adults giggled at Gazelle's instructions. 'Let me show you how to skate and make the very best of your new indoor play-ground. So let's start by moving forward, slowly. Follow me . . .' Shamir, Leanne, Paige, and me all trailed after Gazelle like sheep. 'And . . . turn around. That's right, don't collide,' Gazelle advised. 'Skate back and let's try a figure of eight.'

A figure of eight? You are joking—I couldn't even do a figure of *one*.

Shamir

These cameras, they was trying to film us skating, you know, specially me and my mate Finlay cos we was struggling. But the teachers and the mums kept overtaking us and flinging out their arms like they was film stars and nearly knocking us down. We had to hold on to one another and I felt well daft. Leanne says, this is totally, totally stupid.

Me and my mate Finlay, we stood back against the wall and Finlay says, if they could see themselves, they'd be well shown-up.

Leanne says, it's meant to be us out there, not them.

Paige says, I never thought it'd be like this, did you, Leanne?

The teachers ruin everything, I says, and my mate Finlay says, that's what teachers are there for.

Leanne says, dead sad like, it don't look like we'll get our perfect school.

No. When all them cameras and fancy telly people have gone, they'll all be dead bad-tempered and narky again. Just watch.

The polished woody smell of the new hall surface crept up my nose and kept making me sneeze as we skated around. 'Can't you stop that?' Evergreen asked in a really irritated voice. 'It's not good television, you know.'

'Sorry,' I said.

'It's not Leanne's fault,' Paige responded, annoyed. 'No one can help sneezing.' But Evergreen didn't listen, she skated off in a haughty way.

I stood back against the wall bars with Paige, Finlay, and Shamir and watched the teachers and parents glide around the room with Gazelle.

Standing there, watching the skaters, I was thinking about the week. This was our last day. Things should be almost perfect by this stage, I thought. We *should* have a perfect classroom, sensational dining room, delicious dinners, and wonderful teachers. Well . . . the classroom was different, but as for the rest . . .

Shamir

Then the bell goes for lunchtime and all the kids pour out of their classrooms and start running outside the hall and pressing their faces against the windows and watching us, and Evergreen's going, Get away! and banging on the glass. But the kids don't move their squashed-up noses at all. They're just killing themselves laughing at Mrs Mazurka and Mrs Whitburn and Mrs Towers making right fools of themselves.

I found it hard to say much to anyone at dinner time. Finlay, Shamir, Paige, and I sat in our concrete corner of the playground and talked about the ridiculous episode of the roller skating. Suddenly Finlay said, 'Cor— have you seen that motor?' He was pointing to a sleek black stretched limo parking next to the school gates.

'Look who's here!' Shamir shouted.

Lots of faces turned towards the road as two huge smiles emerged from the back of the car. Suddenly, everyone began charging towards the gates to welcome the new arrivals—Heaven and Devon, the *Perfect Schools* presenters. Mrs Towers was shouting, 'Get back here!' but nobody could hear because the noise of the cheering drowned out her words. 'I said, get back in here!' Still nobody took any notice. Mrs Mazurka wasn't worried about the children's behaviour because *she* was running down to the school gates, too.

'Leanne and gang!' Evergreen shouted. She pushed her way through the cheering children and encouraged us to follow her. It was hard going. Mrs Towers was still yelling at the kids to get back. Then, suddenly, *she* stopped shouting and started running down towards the gates with the rest of the school.

Mrs Mazurka had reached the car but instead of asking everyone to form an orderly line and walk to the playground or something sensible like that, she reached out to Heaven and Devon. 'Hi! It's lovely to welcome you back,' Mrs Mazurka gushed. 'I'm the headteacher, remember?'

'Yeah!' Heaven screeched. 'Although you look

far too young and cool to be a headmistress.' Mrs Mazurka beamed.

'Can't you move the kids back?' Evergreen asked, glaring at Mrs Mazurka.

'That's Mrs Towers's job,' Mrs Mazurka said, brightly. 'Mrs Towers, could you take the children back towards the school?'

Mrs Towers elbowed her way through the crowd. Her face was red and shiny with the effort of all the pushing. She looked totally stupid as she brushed the hair from her face and swung her head back like a show pony. 'Yes, I'm Mrs Towers, the midday supervisor and I'm so thrilled to meet you and be part of such an important occasion. Isn't it amazing how children behave when . . .'

'Oh, for goodness' sake, Mrs Towers!' Mrs Mazurka snapped. She almost sounded jealous. 'I suppose I'll have to do something, then. Children!' she called in a shrill voice.

Everyone ignored her. They kept pushing forward and shouting, 'Heaven! Devon! Over here!' and, 'Can I have your autograph,' and, 'Hello, Mum!' because the cameras were filming.

'Children!' Mrs Mazurka called again and clapped her hands in a pathetic gesture to gain control. She turned to smile at Heaven and Devon. 'One word from me and they do as they please,' she said, laughing.

'This is dreadful,' Evergreen said. 'Why doesn't she do something?'

But Mrs Mazurka hardly noticed the chaos. She kept moving around to watch where the cameras were and smiling at them. Mrs Towers was standing close to her and smiling a manic, star-struck smile constantly. Mrs Whitburn and Mrs Ridley stood behind the excited children, awaiting their turn to be introduced to the presenters.

Then the photographer arrived from the local newspaper and kids were tapping him on the shoulder and saying, 'Take a picture of me, mister,' or, 'My mum buys the paper every day so will you put me in it?'

Behind the photographer was the Lord Mayor and his Lady Mayoress all dressed in their posh clothes and chains. 'Thank you so much for inviting us, Mrs Mazurka,' the Lord

Mayor called above the chaos. 'Now, where would you like us to stand for the photo?'

'I invited you actually, guv'nor,' the photographer said. 'Thought it might add a little civic dignity to the occasion, if you know what I mean.'

'Yes,' the mayor replied, doubtfully. 'So, where shall I stand, Mrs Mazurka?'

Mrs Mazurka shrugged her shoulders. 'Don't ask me. I'm not in charge this afternoon.' She turned to face the camera again. The Lord Mayor and Lady Mayoress both looked astonished.

'This is terrible. What can we do?' Evergreen asked desperately. 'Leanne?'

'I don't know,' I said.

'Say they can have something to eat,' Shamir suggested.

'They've just had their dinner,' Evergreen replied.

'Yeah—but they'll still be hungry,' Finlay said. 'Say something like, "Burger and chips for everyone in the dining room".'

'I don't think that's a very healthy treat,' Paige remarked. 'My mum says that . . .'

'I think you're right, young lady,' the Lord Mayor agreed.

'Leanne?' Paige asked. 'What do you think? Don't you think burgers are a bit unhealthy?'

'Leanne?' Shamir said.

'Leanne?' Finlay shook my elbow.

For a few moments I couldn't say anything. I was so full of anger and embarrassment at Mrs Mazurka and Mrs Towers. They had ruined everything. Why didn't *they* do something? It wasn't our responsibility to control the other kids.

'What's up, Leanne?' Paige asked quietly.

I took a deep breath, trying to control my fury. 'This is rubbish!' I hissed.

'What?' Evergreen questioned.

'This is rubbish!' I shouted at the very top of my voice. 'Absolute rubbish!'

Everything stopped. Everyone turned and stared. At me. Well, it was true. It *was* rubbish.

Mrs Ridley stared at me, for what seemed like an age. She took the whistle from her kaftan pocket and blew loudly. Then she said, 'Excitement over, children! Now I want you to go back to the playground and line up in your class groups and return to your classrooms.' She blew the whistle again. 'Mrs Marsh's class lead on!' Like robots, we marched away from Heaven and Devon.

'Leanne and co.,' Evergreen called.

I looked at Mrs Ridley. 'It's OK,' she said gently. 'Go and finish it off, Leanne.'

'But . . .' I protested. I didn't want to have anything more to do with it. It was a total shambles.

Evergreen folded her arms and leaned towards me, breathing quickly. Her mouth was fixed in a surly sort of grin. She looked so different to the person we had shown round the school all those weeks ago. 'May I remind you, Leanne, my little drama queen,' she said, in a harsh tone, 'you volunteered for this. You weren't forced into it. You may not be happy about it but you must *finish* what you've *started*. Got it?'

LEANNE: FRIDAY EVENING

So we finished it off. Evergreen started fretting and flustering. 'What are we going to do?' she asked, despairingly. 'We can't use this, this is a disaster.'

Devon put his arm around Evergreen. 'Calm down, darling. Just cut the bad bits and film some more.'

'Yeah,' Heaven agreed. 'Just cut out the rubbish bits.'

'You're right,' Evergreen said, smiling. 'OK, we'll cut to the dining room.'

I felt like crying. Just cut out the rubbish bits. What did that mean? Did she mean the bits that we'd done?

We walked over to the dining room. Paige linked arms with me on one side and then Finlay did the same on my other arm which was a massive surprise because boys don't normally do things like that. Shamir put a matey kind of arm around Finlay's shoulder. I caught our reflection in the dining room window and I thought, we're a team, and that made me feel just a little bit better. In the dining room, Evergreen placed us in-between Heaven and Devon, in front of the pastel stripes and asked, 'How do you feel about your Perfect School, Leanne?'

'To be honest, I feel a bit disappointed,' I said in a dead, quiet voice.

'What?' Evergreen shrieked. Heaven smiled like she does when she's talking to kids with broken heads.

'The cameras are on,' Paige said, looking very embarrassed.

'I don't care!' I shouted. 'Why should I care? It's all ruined! It isn't what I expected at all.'

'Leanne, I think you're being just a bit melodramatic,' Evergreen said. 'The week has been a tremendous success . . .'

'No, it hasn't,' I replied. 'We haven't done half of what we wanted and . . . this is supposed to be something for the kids. To make our lives better at school!'

Evergreen glared at me as if I'd gone

mad. 'Nobody has ever been like this before,' she muttered. Then she took a deep breath and said, 'It's not going to be like you think it is, you know. We cut lots of stuff out and in the end it looks, you know . . . like, I don't know, like it's you kids that are doing everything and as if . . . the school's tons better than it was before.'

'Even though you haven't used our ideas? Even though the kids haven't done everything?' I asked. 'And even though it isn't tons better?'

'It will *look* tons better and it will look like it's all your ideas, when it's finished,' Evergreen explained. 'It's all smoke and mirrors, television, nothing is real. So long as our *programme* is perfect.'

So that was it. It wasn't really about making our school into the Perfect School. It wasn't about that at all. They weren't even trying to make a Perfect School. We were trying to do that. *They* were here to make a Perfect Programme.

I should have realized.

17
Back To Normal

'I have got some brilliant ideas for turning our school into the Perfect School. I watch all those makeover programmes on telly and my nan buys all the magazines for doing up old houses. She lives just round the corner from school and her house is like a little palace.

There are lots of things that need changing and sorting out in our school and it would be so brilliant if you could come in and make us into a Perfect School.'

When I wrote my letter, during the summer holidays, I honestly believed that it was possible to make a Perfect School in a week. But it isn't.

My nan has been working on her little house for years and still, she says, it's not perfect.

Things returned to normal very quickly. We had an extremely boring assembly on the Monday after and the first Monday after half-term, the bagpipe music returned. Mrs Mazurka was different, though. She was very quiet and sort of disappointed at first when the week was over. But bit by bit, she is changing. She's wearing her trendy gear again and even bringing her guitar into school. Last Monday when we were all gathered into the hall she made an announcement. 'You know, kids, I've really had enough of these tedious assemblies. I think we should have a singing and fun hour on Fridays instead.'

'Excellent!' Finlay cried.

'Glad you approve, Finlay,' Mrs Mazurka said with a smile. 'So next Friday, I'll bring my guitar into school.'

'Yes!' we said together.

Mrs Ridley has changed, too. She isn't like an angry Victorian teacher any more. She told us about splitting up with her husband and how that had made her so angry and resentful. 'To be honest, children, I've been cross for about five years but now I realize that I have to start a new phase in my life.'

'Been there,' Paige and I said together.

'Didn't think you girls were old enough to get married,' Mrs Ridley said, smiling.

'You know what I mean, Miss,' Paige added. 'Forty per cent of the people in our class have been through what you're going through.'

'Anyway,' Mrs Ridley said, 'that time-out with Devalera Duffy was great for me to realize where *I* had been going wrong with *my* class. So, I want to help make things much better for you.'

And that's what Mrs Ridley did. She listened to our suggestions and helped us put them into practice. That was one good thing about the TV programme, the change in Mrs Ridley.

The playground was a lot less crowded and there weren't as many arguments, mainly because of Finlay's idea. 'Why don't we set up some clubs so that people can do stuff inside at dinner time? What about a *roller skating* club?' he suggested. 'I know it was one of their ideas but we could do it a bit differently. Say, we have *one* teacher and only twenty kids and me and my mate Shamir can be in charge.' Finlay and Shamir set it up by themselves, making badges and ID cards for the members. So many pupils want to join that they've had to make a waiting list.

Paige and I have started a School Improvement Club and during the spring half-term holiday, we're going to repaint the dining room—using Shamir's ideas. We've already chosen the exact shades from one of Nan's colour cards. Nan has said she'll teach me and Paige, Finlay and Shamir how to transform the room. We're going to move some of the big plants down there because they're not all that practical in our classroom. Mrs Ridley can't see everyone when she's talking to the whole class and, as Shamir says, 'We can get up to some right tricks behind them leaves!'

I would love to say that Mrs Whitburn's cooking has improved but it hasn't. She still gets cross when Shamir asks her about the veggie option but then she says, with a smile, 'If you're not careful, I'll start cooking some of that Jamie D'Ollio rubbish.'

'Jimmy!' Finlay reminds her and that really makes her laugh.

After we all saw a video of the finished programme, (which made everything look fantastic—smoke and mirrors as Evergreen said!) Mrs Towers's life took a dramatic turn. She was so thrilled with being on the telly that she resigned from her job and joined an agency which provides extras for films and television programmes. My nan got the job as the new dinner lady. She says that it gets her out of the house! She's been brilliant, teaching us old-fashioned skipping games and things like that. She says that we should celebrate the fact that ours is a Victorian school.

In the summer term we're going to have a Victorian day where we all dress in the clothes of the time and play some of the games Nan has taught us. Mrs Whitburn says she might even cook us some Victorian food. (*No change there*, Shamir says.)

Sometimes, when I sit in the concrete corner of the playground, I gaze up at the red-brick school building and I feel so proud of what *we* have done to improve our school: Finlay, Shamir, Paige, and me, our team. It wasn't Evergreen and her team who have changed things. It was *us*.

Way back in the heat of September, Mrs Mazurka was right about one thing—this year is going to be the best ever for our school, Venus Crescent Primary.

Also by Josephine Feeney

So, You Want to be the Perfect Family?

Are you happy with your family?

If not, would you like to change it?

Would you let television cameras into your home to record these changes?

We are searching for a family to transform into the PERFECT FAMILY . . .

Call this number NOW!

Katie doesn't think her family are too bad.
But they're not perfect. So this TV show
is the chance of a lifetime. But can the
experts really make them perfect?

And do they want everybody watching
while they do it?

ISBN 0 19 275233 2

Josephine Feeney was born in Leicester in 1956 and has seven brothers and sisters. Her parents both come from the west of Ireland. On leaving school she trained to be a special needs teacher. She had been writing since she was at school, and while teaching in Yorkshire she attended a writers' group and started to write seriously. In 1987 she moved to Essex and had her first radio play accepted by the BBC. She then moved back to Leicester to take up writing full time and had her first novel published in 1994. She is married, with two children, and in her spare time she enjoys listening to music, playing her accordion, and going on picnics to her allotment. *Makeover Madness* is her second book for Oxford University Press.